Whoever degrades another degrades me, and whatever is done or said returns at last to me.
—Walt Whitman

I am a soldier, not a politician, and I am not equipped to debate moral issues. I do know that what happens to our politicians happens to all of us, and the cannibals are trying to devour them. I can't allow that. Hell, I *will not* allow that.
—Mack Bolan, THE EXECUTIONER

THE EXECUTIONER:
Washington I.O.U.

by
Don Pendleton

PINNACLE BOOKS • NEW YORK CITY

DEDICATION:

To the honest men,
the ethical men,
the dedicated men . . .
wherever the hell they may be.

PROLOGUE

It had already earned him fame as "the Executioner" in the war zones of Southeast Asia when Mack Bolan's spectacular brand of warfare was suddenly transplanted to the city streets of his homeland.

As a U.S. Army sergeant, Bolan's combat excellence was built of many commendable attributes. His military superiors regarded him as "a natural soldier." He seemed to possess an almost intuitive "feel" for combat tactics and strategies. He was rated an expert marksman with virtually every personal weapon in the army's arsenal. On penetration strikes into enemy-held territory, Bolan had repeatedly demonstrated a cool self-sufficiency, nerves of steel, and the ability to complete missions despite overwhelming obstacles.

In a modern army heavy on specialties, Mack Bolan practiced the oldest specialty in the book of warfare. He was a death specialist. During two tours of combat duty in Vietnam, he had "executed" ninety-seven enemy VIPs, by confirmed count, and he had come to be regarded as a formidable weapon in the army's psychological warfare efforts.

7

And then Sgt. Bolan experienced a personal trage-
dy. He was called home on emergency leave to make
burial arrangements for his father, mother, and teen-
age sister—all victims of violent death. When he
learned that the local Mafia arm was responsible for
the triple-tradgedy, Mack Bolan seceded from the
Asian wars and turned his attention to "the home
front."

"It looks like I have been fighting the wrong enemy," the sergeant wrote in his personal journal. "Why
defend a front line 8,000 miles away when the *real*
enemy is chewing up everything you love back home?
I have talked to the police about this situation and
they seem to be helpless to do anything. The problem, as I see it, is that the rules of warfare are all
rigged against the cops. Just *knowing* the enemy isn't
enough. They have to *prove* he's the enemy, and even
then sometimes he slips away from them. What is
needed here is a bit of direct action, strategically
planned, and to hell with the rules. Over in 'Nam, we
called it a war of attrition. Seek out and destroy.
Exterminate the enemy. I guess it's time a war was
declared on the home front. The same kind of war
we've been fighting at 'Nam. The very same kind."

Mack Bolan, indeed, declared a personal war on
the Mafia. It was not to be a limited war, not in any
sense. It was to be "*war everlasting*"—that is, everlasting in terms of Bolan's own lifetime.

This competent combat veteran held no illusions
regarding the eventual outcome of such a war. He
knew what the odds were. It was obvious that he

would be fighting the impossible fight. There could be but one logical conclusion: the death of Mack Bolan.

Even so, he infiltrated the enemy camp in his home town, Pittsfield, and began his cool campaign of identification and destruction. Much to his own surprise, Bolan emerged victorious from that initial skirmish, and when he left Pittsfield *that* Mafia arm was a shambles.

The Executioner was strongly aware, however, that all trails away from Pittsfield were, in effect, his "last mile" of life. He vowed to make it a bloody mile and to make each step along that wipeout trail as costly as possible to the enemy. He would not "roll over and die for them."

He then declared the entire underworld a jungle—an arena in which the only law was survival of the fittest—and his war became a series of guerilla campaigns. Wherever he surfaced, hell broke loose; wherever he lingered, ruin and destruction descended upon the enemy. Before long, the lordly masters of organized crime throughout the nation were beginning to address themselves to "the Bolan problem" with the gravest respect.

An "open contract" was issued against the life of this blitzing one-man army, with the initial $100,000 bounty on his head pyramiding into astronomical amounts as local chieftains hastily added "area bonuses" in an attempt to discourage Executioner strikes in their territories.

Meanwhile law enforcement agencies at every

level of government throughout the nation were viewing Mack Bolan's one-man anti-crime crusade with growing alarm, and a tight "Bolan watch" was being federally coordinated toward the apprehension of this "highly dangerous" fugitive. Even internationally, Bolan was a wanted man. Interpol as well as national police in several European nations had reasons for an interest in the activities of the Executioner.

Thus it must have seemed that every hand was raised against him. Bolan had not, however, expected to be decorated for his actions in this new application of warfare. He had known from the beginning that his campaign would be officially regarded as both immoral and illegal; he was prepared to accept the condemnation of his society. He even accepted philosophically the knowledge that many police agencies were observing an unofficial "shoot on sight—shoot to kill" policy in their attempts to apprehend him.

From Bolan's viewpoint, though, the police were not his enemy. He studiously avoided any confrontation with police authority and he had never been known to exchange gunfire or hostilities of any nature with the law enforcement establishment.

Actually, many police officers were secretly sympathetic to Bolan's war, and it is felt that frequently individual policemen "turned their backs" and consciously avoided confrontations with the blitzing warrior. It is known that Bolan's closest friend and contact within the establishment was an undercover agent who was also high in the crime syndicate's hierarchy. Another Bolan intelligence contact was a highly placed official in the U.S. Justice Department. Neither of these contacts was on an official basis, however, and rumors that Bolan was being financed and otherwise supported by various governmental agencies are patently false.

Bolan financed his own war, via raids on the enemy's money caches. From the beginning, he seemed to delight in "hitting them where it hurts"—in their money pipelines, their "clout routes" (bribery networks for political influence), and in their juicy semi-legitimate business covers. He had learned early in the wars that the enemy's seeming omnipotence was derived mainly from the power of their great wealth—from their "bought" politicians, law-officials, legal-eagles and unscrupulous businessmen.

The actual source of their power, though, was quickly seen as the common everyday moral weakness of mass America. The Mafia's billions come from the dimes and dollars harvested daily through organized gambling, prostitution, loan-sharking, bootlegging, narcotics and other mass-interest sources of illegal revenue.

But Bolan was no moralist and his war was not directed against the common weaknesses of mankind. His war was with the Mafia itself, which he saw as a ravenous leech at the throat of his nation, a monster bloated fantastically by an insatiable appetite for wealth and power, a nightmarish crime cartel with

11

tentacles wriggling out in all directions in a determination to encompass the world.

His first brush with the mob's political ambitions came in New York where he learned that *La Cosa Nostra* (translated literally, Our Thing, or this thing of ours) was giving birth to an even more formidable *Cosa di tutti Cosi*, the Thing of all Things, a movement described by worried government officials as "the nation's invisible second government."

The new Thing was spreading like a cancerous growth into the financial and political institutions of the country—indeed, of the entire world—and it was at Chicago that Bolan saw that the festering pool of politics lent the most natural environment for the growth and perpetuation of the monster. It was in Chicago that he gained personal insights into the power structure of a society in which the businessman is a politician, the politician is a criminal and the criminal is a businessman.

This "unholy trinity" came into sharp focus at Las Vegas, where untold millions of "skim" dollars moved steadily from the green-felt gold mines to the graft-lined halls of government and finance everywhere. It was an unending stream—and Bolan himself flowed along one such underground river to the sunny Caribbean playgrounds, into a personal experience with the syndicate's international intentions.

It was during the Caribe strike that Bolan formed a sketchy understanding of that brooding conglomerate which he termed "the Fourth Power"—an international apolitical force which was bent on world domination—and it was this understanding which launched him into an invasion of the mob's western U.S. trade routes.

In San Francisco Bolan found the confrontation with Fourth Power plans which solidified in his mind the full implications of the unholy alliance—a combine whose only allegiance was to the buck; whose only politics was power; whose only morality was built of corruption, greed and rapacity.

The Executioner's call on Boston was for purely personal business, but even this emergency mission developed into another head-on collision with the syndicate's master plan for unlimited power—and this was the collision which sent Bolan richocheting into Washington for a sweep of the national clout routes.

Bolan found the smell of Mafia hanging heavy in the Washington atmosphere. A series of ominous events had been taking place in and around the national capital, but they were not political events in the usual sense.

Obscure but important officials in key governmental positions had been victims of mortal "accidents"—more than a half-dozen in the past few months. Others had quietly disappeared from the scene—"missing" without a trace. A few had simply resigned abruptly—taken "normal" departures.

Occuring over a period of several months, the events seemed unrelated and without unitary significance except in the minds of a few worried observers of the Washington scene—and even these few hesitated to use the word "conspiracy" to explain the rapidly changing picture of official Washington.

There was no hesitation on Bolan's part, however. No other man outside the mob's top ruling circle has been so close to the reality of *La Cosa Nostra* and the newly developed concept of *Cosa di tutte le Cose*. The Executioner has inside information pointing definitely to a mob conspiracy in the hub of the nation's government—and The Thing of all Things has never seemed more probable as an existent force in American life.

Bolan had hoped from the beginning to keep his war a simple one. His avowed intention had been to "hit and keep hitting until I shake their house down around them." The complications had set in early, however, the audacious warrior had been aware of a steady broadening of the battle fronts.

In Washington he is destined to discover that the focus of his entire life has become pinpointed at this nerve center of America.

"It's my country," he wrote in his journal on the eve of his sweep into Washington. "It's not perfect, but it's the best I've ever seen ... and I've seen a few. I left a lot of buddies behind in 'Nam, guys who will never see home again. So, yeah, this one is going to be sheer hell. But I owe it. I owe it to the guys who won't be coming home. I can't let the mob swagger away with this nation's government in their hip pockets.

"A lot of blood has been spilled in the defense of this country. Even if the country itself is not sacred, that spilt blood sure as hell is. So what choice do I have, except to spill some more. So this one is for the

14

beloved dead. Let's call it the Washington IOU. And let the mob pay the tab ... with their blood."

The Executioner's battle plans were set, and the strike on Washington was under way.

1: THE GAME

The woman jumped out of her vehicle before it was fully parked and ran smack into the waiting arms of Horse Lucchese and Tommy the Sandman Roberts, two of the meanest hitmen in Washington. Without even a hello or by-your-leave the enforcers grabbed the flustered beauty and roughly hustled her into the shadows at the side of the apartment building.

Bolan left his car at the curb out front and flitted along in quiet pursuit, making full use of the natural cover of darkness and closing just enough to maintain visual contact.

Obviously something had gone sour and the Executioner wanted to know precisely what that something was.

He'd been on Claudia Vitale's tail for nearly a week, dogging her around Washington on an eighteen-hour a day surveillance—and she had been a very busy little bagwoman for the Capital mob.

Bolan did not ordinarily devote so much time and attention to a payoff courier—he either hit them or forgot them. But this one was something else. Dropping bags around venal Washington was just a moon-lighting sideline for Mrs. Vitale. At the stroke of eight every morning she turned back into the sedate and capable Chief Administrative Aide to the venerable old patriarch of Capitol Hill, Congressman Harmon Keel.

And, yeah, this made Claudia Vitale a very special item in Mack Bolan's book of warfare.

She didn't actually tote payroll bags around Cloutville, of course. What she carried were tidy little envelopes which could be inconspicuously passed at bureaucratic gatherings and social-set happenings.

Bolan's chief interest had lain in the recipients of those envelopes.

Not that the courier herself was unworthy of a man's interest. She was the kind who was never in-conspicuous, whatever the crowd. Belled hips, allur-ingly sloped in the upper approaches and firmly rounded at the bases. Long legs, exquisitely tapered from full thighs—all of it together. A nipped little waist exploding upwards toward softly voluptuous womanhood and delicately molded shoulders. Swan neck, smooth as velvet and gracefully supporting a head of classic Roman beauty.

On those evening rounds, she looked more like a Washington VIP-league call girl; Bolan had to wonder if she'd once doubled in that capacity, also.

She'd been an easy mark to watch. Bolan could spot her walk from a block away. He knew all the little gestures as she conversed or dined or sipped at a cocktail. She was highly animated, a very much

18

alive and interesting woman. He had been close enough often enough to know the flash and sparkle of those dark eyes, and he could tell by the tilt of her head if she was bored, interested, sad or mad.

Right now, at the tired end of this evening, Bolan's reading on Claudia Vitale was that she was "scared out of her skull."

And with damned good reason. The Horse and the Sandman were not particularly known for polite conversation and social graces.

They had maneuvered the woman to the rear entrance of the building. ... Bolan knew where they were headed. He doubled back, went in through the front door—delayed only momentarily by the efficient security locks—and proceeded directly to the top floor. He emerged from the elevator just in time to see the others disappearing inside the Vitale apartment.

Something about the look on the woman's face as the Sandman shoved her through that doorway struck a sympathetic chord in Bolan's mind. He decided to go in for a direct reading ... but not without a quick recon of the battle zone.

The Executioner quietly backtracked his own route to the ground level, then went to the rear exit and let himself outside. He stood on the small porch for a moment, casually lit a cigarette while his eyes probed the dimly-lit parking area.

He scored immediately, finding the thing he'd expected to find.

The outside man.

He was seated tensely at the wheel of a Pontiac

LeMans, a beefy man with a nervous cigar. The parking lights were on and the engine was running, the vehicle parked rear-end to the building and ready for a fast departure.

Hell, it was a setup for a hit.

Bolan went on down the steps and walked directly to the Pontiac. The guy's eyes were following his progress with a curious and indecisive stare.

Bolan stepped right up and tapped on the window. It rolled down immediately and the stereo sounds of a tape deck drifted through the opening.

The Executioner's ominously-tipped Beretta Belle drifted in, attaching herself to a point directly between a pair of suddenly-flaring eyes. She coughed once, quietly and almost apologetically, and death whispered in between those eyes and shuttered them forever.

Bolan opened the door and eased the messy remains onto the floorboards, then he turned off the ignition and the lights, rolled up the window, locked and closed the door, and went back to where the action was.

The apartment door yielded to the first delicate probe. Bolan swept on inside.

All the lights were on. The woman's handbag was lying on the floor just inside the door. It was nice, simply decorated but reeking of affluence—sliding glass doors at the end of the living room, small balcony outside, Washington Monument visible in the background.

A large TV-stereo combo served also as a bar, but there was no action there.

An open doorway led to the bedroom, also brightly lighted. The shimmering cocktail gown the woman had been wearing was now lying in a wad just inside the door; other, more intimate articles, were strung along in an erratic path to the bathroom. That door was partially closed. The unmistakable sounds of a bathtub being filled with water were the only sounds in the place.

They had not, Bolan knew, rushed up here for a quick community bath.

He hit the door with a commanding foot, sending it banging into the party, the Belle close behind and at the ready.

Horse Lucchese caught the full force of that moving door and he went over head first into the tub with a startled cry.

The Beretta's whispering death overtook him there, two of her grim little messengers plowing into the rear of the gunner's skull at cerebellum level to liberate bubbling blood and jellied matter into the swiftly discoloring water.

The other guy had his hands full of Claudia Vitale. She was very nude and putting up one hell of a grim fight for her life. The Sandman was scratched and bleeding about the face; both of them were so preoccupied with their own troubles that they were not immediately aware of the new presence in the Vitale bathroom.

Roberts was the first to know, via the unsettling

thing in the bathtub. He froze for a split-second, then gave the woman a panicky shove toward the far wall and came around in a fast pivot, clawing gunleather.

The silent Beretta tracked right along with him, and Tommy the Sandman kept right on going round, collecting Parabellum hi-shockers in the head and throat as he spun onto the john, then slid into a deflated heap, wedged between the porcelain fixture and the wall, dead eyes open and reflecting the bewilderment of that final instant of life.

Bolan stepped inside and turned off the bath water.

The woman was slumped against the far wall, one arm raised and steadying herself against the corner, the other pressed flat to the wall beside her as though she were trying to hold it upright. Horrified eyes rebounded from the mess in her bathroom and she moaned, "Oh God. . . ."

Bolan growled, "Get out of here."

"They fed me p-pills," she gasped, " . . . sleeping pills. Going to drown me. Make it look . . . accident. Already taking effect I guess."

One knee buckled and she almost went down.

Bolan snatched a large bath towel from a wall rack and draped it over her shoulders as he grabbed her and pulled her out of there. "How many pills did you take?" he asked her.

"Too many," she replied weakly.

She had her eyes on the bed but Bolan pulled her on into the kitchen and bent her over the sink. "Stick a finger down your throat," he gruffly commanded.

22

"There hasn't been time for that stuff to get into your system."

"You're wrong," she protested. "I can feel it."

"What you're feeling is Tommy the Sandman and Horse Lucchese," Bolan told her. "Now whose finger is it going to be, yours or mine?"

She swiveled her head about and those dark eyes probed his briefly before she asked, "Do I know you?"

The towel fell to the floor.

Bolan stared at her for a moment, taking in all there was to take. There was quite a bit, then he retrieved the towel and knotted it about her waist as he told her, "You're going to. I'm Mack Bolan."

The eyes receded somewhat and a curtain seemed to fall into place there. In a very tired voice she said, "That's all it takes to make my night." Then she turned back to the sink and muttered, "For what it's worth, thanks for my life. Now go away; leave my misery private."

He instructed her anyhow, "If the finger doesn't work, try some salt water. But get it up, empty the stomach completely. Then make some strong coffee and fill your belly with it. Wet the towel and slap yourself in the face with it if you're feeling drowsy. And stay on your feet."

"Okay, okay," she whispered.

Bolan returned to the slaughterhouse.

Blood was spattered across the walls, and pools of it were oozing across the floor tiles. He threw some towels down, then he took two sheets from the linen closet and ripped away the laundry marks. He wrapped the corpses in tight shrouds and stuffed in heavy towels to absorb the leakage.

He heard Claudia Vitale retching in the kitchen as he carried Tommy the Sandman through the apartment.

The time was two o'clock. The quiet Georgetown neighborhood was wrapped up for the night, so there seemed little danger of being discovered with his grisly burden.

On the second trip he found the woman standing quietly in the kitchen doorway, the towel draped around her, sarong fashion, patting her face with an ice cube.

"What are you doing with them?" she asked in a solemn tone.

"Taking them home," he growled.

Horse Lucchese was draped over his shoulder. Bolan gave the woman a reassuring wink and went on about his business. He took the elevator down and exited through the rear, depositing Horse in the Pontiac with the other two. He dropped his calling card, a marksman's medal, into the pile-up of lifeless flesh and drove the cargo to an address just a few blocks away. He parked the Pontiac in a no-parking zone at the front of a renovated brownstone and dropped the keys into the mail box. Then he returned on foot to the scene of the hit and moved his own car to the parking slot in which the Pontiac had been standing.

Claudia Vitale's door was safety-locked, bolted

24

from the inside. He went on to the roof, locating an easy access to the balcony outside her apartment.

The lock on the glass doors yielded easily to the pressure of his blade. He found the woman in the bedroom. She was wearing a frilly dressing gown and she was seated cross-legged in the middle of the bed, sharing it with a half-packed suitcase.

She had one of those toy-like .25 calibre autoloaders in her hand. She was making a point of showing it to him.

Quietly he told her, "Go for the throat if you intend to make any score with that thing."

Her eyes were luminous and regretful, her head tilted into a sad attitude. "I don't know just how to take you, Mr. Bolan," she said solemnly.

"I don't want your head, Mrs. Vitale." He stood quite still and snapped a glance toward the suitcase. "Good idea. Finish your packing. If they've decided to hit you, a momentary setback won't change anything. Every breath you draw now is a stolen one."

She gave a tremulous sigh and replied, "I know. Maybe you shouldn't have butted in. It would all be over now."

Bolan shrugged. "That's one way of looking at it."

"Why did you? Butt in, I mean. What are you looking for in Washington?"

"I'm looking for the man."

She sighed again. "What man?"

He batted the question away with a flick of the eyes. "Why were the boys hitting you?"

She countered with: "Do you know who I am? I mean . . ."

He assured her, "I know. I've been living with you for five days."

A tense silence took control of the atmosphere between them. Presently Dolan suggested, "You're pointing the gun at the wrong guy."

Her gaze fell away from his. She dropped the little weapon to the bed and lowered her face into her hands. "I guess it doesn't matter," she said in a weary, muffled voice. "Why'd you save me?"

He replied, "I don't know. Why were they hitting you?"

All the fight had apparently drained from her. She gave the lovely head a dismal shake, still holding it in her hands, and told him, "Gang war, maybe. Who knows?"

He said, "Huh-uh, try again. Why were Carlo Spinella's boys putting you away?"

She hesitated, then dropped the hands and tilted her head to meet his gaze as she replied, "Let's just say I was getting tired of the game."

"Okay."

"The game of crud. Capitol Crud."

"That's the one," Bolan said. A smile flickered briefly across that cold face. "Aside from Congressman Keel, who gives you your orders?"

Dully, she replied, "Leave Harmon Keel out of it. That poor old man hasn't given an order to anybody in years. He seldom knows what day it is. We prop him up, send him out and pray he finds his way back home again."

Bolan already knew that. He continued the probing. "Who is Lupo?"

The woman did not respond.

He tried again. "That's Italian for *wolf*. It's a code name, isn't it? Who is Lupo?"

Very quietly she told him to go to hell.

He ignored that and told her, "I guess you heard that Al 88 is dead."

"Al who?"

"You know who. They buried him in Boston a few days ago, as Albert Greene." Bolan produced a small notebook and riffled the pages. "His personal file was lousy with the names Lupo, Keel, and Vitale."

She said, "So?"

"So ... Al is dead. Vitale was meant to be dead. That leaves only Lupo and Keel. Which one has the most reason to want the other one dead, Mrs. Vitale?"

She asked him, "Do you have a cigarette?"

He lit a Pall Mall and gave it to her. She took a nervous pull at it, then blew smoke at him with a long-drawn sigh. "It's certainly not Keel," she declared, sighing in resignation. "I told you. He's almost eighty years old. Hasn't had a new thought of his own for at least the past five."

"And you've been the real power behind the man," Bolan suggested.

She shook her head. "I've just been the control link. Until a few months ago, Mr. Castiglione ... you know Mr. Castiglione?"

Bolan said, "I executed him."

"That's right," she replied with a rueful wrinkling of the pert nose, "you did do that. Well, until then, Castiglione was running the Keel machine, through yours truly. The Washington end, at least. I got the job after ... after. ..."

"After your husband was gunned down," Bolan suggested.

"Yes." Her voice had become hardly more than a whisper. "Well ... then ... Lupo stepped into the picture, replacing Castiglione."

Bolan commented, "Big Guss Riappi is supposed to be heir to that throne."

She tossed her head and took another tense pull at the cigarette. "Not the political territory. Those strings are being pulled straight from the national head shed."

"Via Lupo," Bolan said.

"Yes, via Lupo."

"So who is Lupo?"

"Look. I'm not in the organization. I just do what they tell me. They own me body and soul."

"Who is Lupo?"

"I'm trying to tell you, I don't know."

He said, "I think you do."

"You go to hell, then. I'm telling you I've never seen the man. This is real cloak and dagger stuff. I've heard his voice, muffled and disguised I'm sure, on the phone. That's all. I wouldn't know him if he climbed in my bed."

Bolan asked her, "Do you want to stay alive?"

28

She said, "Of course I want to stay alive."

"How would you go about doing that?" he asked quietly.

"I ... don't know. What would you suggest?"

"Play my game for awhile. Maybe we can figure something out, something lasting."

"Your game?"

He showed her a thin smile. "Anti-crud."

Her eyes fell again and she said, "Okay." She handed him the cigarette and dropped onto her back, hands clasped behind her head. Delectably tapered legs dangled over the side of the bed and the dressing gown slid open, revealing, in a more provocative pose, the natural attractions exposed earlier.

She made no move toward recovery. Bolan leaned over her and closed the gown. "That's not part of the game," he said gruffly.

"What did you see?" she asked soberly.

"I saw a hell of a lot of woman," he assured her. "But that—"

"You saw a whore," she quietly corrected him.

So okay, maybe his earlier thoughts about the call-girl angle were pretty close on target.

He tried to tell her that he was not interested in a listing of sins. "That's not—"

"Shut up and let me tell you this. I'm a mob whore. I disguise myself as a legitimate and respected member of the government community, and I seduce reputable and upstanding male members of that same community. I lead them into a set-up where the most vigorous and athletic styles of love-making are strongly encouraged and where hidden motion picture cameras record everything that takes place. Do you understand me?"

Sure, Bolan understood. He could have written the scenario himself, after about the third day of observation of this very interesting subject.

He told her, "So what's new?"

She smiled, genuinely, warmly. "Thanks," she said. "I wanted you to know. And. . . ."

"And what?"

"Well . . . you had to know. If uh, if you were to understand why the goon squad jumped me tonight."

He said, "Go on."

"Lupo has his own enforcers, but he uses the muscle of the local mobsters for the more routine business. My end of it is considered part of the routine. Lupo picks my victims and sics me on them. But then I deliver the evidence to Carlo Spinella. I assume that he takes it from there, applying the pressure to the victim plus whatever muscle may be required. That way, Lupo is never directly involved. As for *me*. . . ."

Bolan said, "You're just one of the victims too, eh?"

She nodded, trying for a smile and failing. "That's the way it usually comes out. I contact my pigeon after he has had time to squirm awhile, and I get hysterical all over the place, insisting that he do whatever has to be done to protect me from being scandalized. It's just another pressure point, but sometimes it's the only thing that will turn the trick. Some of these victims would actually take their lumps rather than submit to blackmail. I guess it eases their

30

conscience to think that they're protecting a woman's honor. Anyway. . . ."

"So why did Spinella's boys jump you?"

"I'm getting to that. All this rotten business started when Lupo appeared on the scene. Before that my job had been purely an administrative routine, contact work, payoffs, lobbying deals, that sort of thing. But Lupo hit this town like a plague. The acceleration has been really intense. They're going for all of it, the whole thing, not just bits and pieces. The really tough nuts—you know, the critical men they couldn't buy, trick, or intimidate—well, those were put on *my* list."

"How many?" Bolan wanted to know.

"All total, I don't know. So far I've destroyed eight of them, with my own special talent. And it became very scary. I mean, look, this always has been a dirty town. The deals, the payoffs, that has been just business as usual for as long as anyone can remember. It's the American system, it simply lends itself to corrupt manipulation. I didn't have too much trouble with my conscience as long as I was just playing the usual Washington games. But *this* . . . well this isn't just politics now. It's actual subversion, it's a coup. The mob is taking it over, all of it, they're taking over the government."

Bolan could have written that scenario, also. Somehow, though, hearing it from this beautiful young woman's lips, the truth hit closer to home and sent an apprehensive shiver along his spine.

"And you couldn't live with that," he muttered.

31

"No, I couldn't. I had another love-nest assignment for tonight. And I just couldn't go through with it."

"Who was the pigeon?"

She gave him a name that quivered his eyelids.

Bolan said, "The White House guy?"

She nodded. "One of the bright young men of the administration, a presidential favorite. We've been setting him up for about two weeks. Tonight was the assignation. I didn't go."

Bolan whistled softly through his teeth. "When you said 'all of it,' you really meant *all* of it, didn't you."

She gave that classic Roman head a saucy tilt and replied, "Where do you think it would all end? I mean, once inside the White House, how much farther would they have to go?"

Vertically, not much farther. Horizontally, though.

. . .

His eyes brooding, Bolan asked her, "Are you the only woman involved in the sex routine?"

"I'm sure I'm not," she told him. "But I drew the big ones because it's so easy for me to move in the various Washington circles. I'm known, you see, because of my position with Harmon Keel. I get invited to all the wing-dings. A lot of men who would never risk an association with an honest-to-God prostitute are just so much ripe meat for a discreet affair with a gal like me." She sat upright and daintily shrugged her shoulders. "You know, men really are quite vulnerable to a routine like mine. I mean, even the greatest men. The Achilles tendon isn't in the heel, you know. It's in the. . . ."

Bolan said, "Yeah," wryly, and moved over to stand beside the window.

"It sounds pretty far out, though," he said musingly, deliberately looking out the window instead of at the girl. "I'm talking about the move against you, now. You sound like a pretty valuable member of the team. I can't see them rubbing you out, not for simply standing up a date."

"Well . . . I guess I did a little more than that," she replied in a small voice. "I guess I tipped my pigeon to the set-up, then I guess I sent him a file on my other eight victims."

Bolan said, "Damn!"

She was gazing at him with a demure smile. "Dumb, you mean."

He met her gaze and replied, "I guess that's what I meant."

She said, "Carlo's goons intercepted the files. You know the rest."

He growled, "Yeah."

"Well . . . where do we go from here?"

"Far away," he grunted. "You'd better get dressed. And finish your packing, but not too much."

She slid off the bed and stood there swaying for a moment while capturing her equilibrium, then she began moving briskly about the bedroom, rounding up clothing and tossing it into the bag. This completed, she slipped out of the gown and hastily pulled on silken underthings while Bolan turned studious attention once more to the window.

The parking lot lay directly below.

His feigned interest in the scene down there took on a genuine tone as the woman asked him, "Should I wear something casual?"

"Suit yourself," he replied. "Just so it's fast. I believe we have new company."

She joined him for a quick peek through the drapes, brushing feminine warmth disturbingly into his awareness, then she made a strangled little sound and dodged back away from the window.

Five guys were spilling out of a large car down there. Two were carrying choppers and another was toting a sawed-off shotgun.

He quietly asked the woman, "Did you send for those dudes?"

"God no!" she snapped, outraged by the suggestion.

He believed her, and that presented another huge question.

There could not have been that quick a reaction to the cargo Bolan had left in front of Carlo Spinella's place. Besides, that crew down there now were no local comedians. They were very obviously nationals, cold professionals who played the Bolan game with an excellence which the Executioner had learned to respect.

They would not be coming for Claudia Vitale, surely, with all that firepower in open display.

On the other hand ... if Claudia had not tipped them during his absence from the apartment, then they should not be aware that Mack Bolan was even on the premises.

So what the hell *had* they come for?

Bolan elected to defer the answer to that question to a better time and place. He scooped up the woman's suitcase and steered her out of there just as she stood, in panties and bra, and they made a strategic withdrawal to the roof.

With a bit of luck and some critical timing, they could be away and gone while the new hit team was fanning through the building.

But the game was set now, of that much Bolan was certain. The first card had been dealt, and the Executioner was into the pot with everything of life he possessed.

He had the dismal feeling, also, that maybe the entire country was in that pot.

The girl had told him, *"They're going for all of it, the whole thing."*

Sure. *Cosa di tutti Cosi*, alive and well in Washington.

What the hell could a man alone hope to accomplish in the face of all that?

It would have to be a highly personal campaign, with each target painstakingly selected. He'd have to hit them in the gut and keep hitting them there until a guard dropped somewhere and he could close in for the killing punch.

So okay, the game was defined.

Find Lupo. Dispose of him.

Hope to God that someone else in this besieged city would find the sense and the guts to join in its defense.

First, of course, he had to get himself out of that

building. And he had to get the girl out. Against five professional hitmen armed with automatic weapons.

So okay, one task at a time.

He pulled Claudia Vitale into a rough embrace and told her, "Get this the first time through because there's no time for repeats and no room for missed signals. This is precisely what you have to do, and both our lives depend on it. First, you drag something out of that bag and put it on. Then, now listen closely, then you. ..."

Yeah, he was in the pot. And with a wild card. Claudia Vitale could very possibly be the largest phony in Washington.

2: THE CREW

They called themselves "the Wolf Crew," and they
could not have been more appropriately named. The
chief was Frank Matti, a thirty-one-year-old ex-
marine who was known in national mob circles as
Gung-ho Matti. He was strong on "image" and he
believed that pride in one's profession was the surest
road to success.

It was an elite crew and they had an important job.
Only Matti was an *omerta* brother, an official member of the secret brotherhood of crime. The other four
crewmembers held employee status, reporting directly to Matti and only to Matti.

Each had been carefullly selected on the basis of
"maturity, efficiency, and experience"—which, translated, meant that they were nerveless assassins who
could be counted on to keep their cool, to take orders, to keep their personal lives "clean," and to keep
their mouths shut.

All were ex-GI's.

Ramon "Bandalero" Vasquez had once been a gunner's mate in the navy. He was a skilled gunsmith and

a car-racing enthusiast. The twenty-eight-year-old Vasquez functioned primarily as the crew's wheelman and weapons specialist.

Billy "Wild Bill" Stewart had seen combat duty in Vietnam with an army rifle company. He was, like Bolan, a sharpshooter with a deadly eye and an ability to function alone. Unlike Bolan, he seemed to have lost whatever abilities he may once have had for "target discrimination"—Wild Bill would shoot anything he was told to shoot, and without a quiver.

Bob Buckholzer and Dan Semple were air force vets. They had met while undergoing training as air police, and they'd been a team ever since. Once they had toured with recruiters, demonstrating the tools of an AP's trade—proficiency with personal weapons, judo, dog handling, etc. The "Apes" were big men, physically excellent, with minds as hard as their bodies. Their crew specialty was muscle, and they enjoyed using it.

The crew functioned with the military precision of a drill team. Each knew his own role to perfection, and he knew how it interacted with the roles of the others. During a "movement" there was seldom any necessity for verbal instructions. They moved quickly, smoothly, quietly—with a minimum of lost motion.

The Wolf Crew, by any normal method of measurement, should have been more than a match for any two men—even two Mack Bolans.

The "movement" on Claudia Vitale's apartment building did not begin, however, as anything more than a routine assignment; the initial approach was a typical one. Bandalero Vasquez pulled the big crew wagon noiselessly into the parking lot, then maneuvered it into an unobstructed exit path.

All four doors opened simultaneously and the Wolf Crew disembarked—Matti and Vasquez from the front, the other three moving fluidly through the rear exits.

Vasquez was carrying his "massive hit" weapon, a sawed-off double-barreled shotgun which he had built himself. He faded into the darkness and took up a concealed defensive position, from which he could assure himself complete coverage of their vehicle.

Matti and Wild Bill Stewart carried Thompsons; they split and took opposite directions in an encirclement of the building while the Apes invaded the building itself from both ends.

It was a routine movement.

Two minutes later Buckholzer reappeared at the front door and summoned his chief with a hand signal.

Matti materialized from the shadows of the building and joined him on the steps for a quiet consultation.

"They were here, all right," the Ape reported in soft tones. "Not now, the joint's empty. But something got butchered in the broad's bathroom."

Matti smoothed his hair with a nervous gesture and replied, "Well, shit. Why'd he wait so late to send us? Where's Danny?"

"Checking topside, just for hell. Waste of time. They split long ago."

"Well, go ahead and run it clear through," Matti instructed. "We'll cover you down here. Hear shooting, come a'running."

Buck the Ape nodded his head and went back upstairs.

The crew chief returned to his position outside, covering the front of the building with his automatic weapon. He had hardly re-settled into the stake-out when a moving object blurred through the upper periphery of his vision and thudded to earth a few feet behind him.

Quiveringly alert, Matti held his cover for a tense moment while eyes and ears scanned the immediate area for another sign of movement. Getting none, he ventured out of the shadows for an inspection of the fallen object, and found himself staring down into the bug-eyed gaze of Danny Semple.

Danny the Ape wasn't looking back, though. Danny would never look at anyone or anything again. And it wasn't the fall from the roof that had killed him. It was the nylon noose, buried deep into the soft flesh of his throat and twisting the face into contortions which even death and a five-story fall could not erase.

Yeah. The Ape had died hard—quick, maybe, but hard and struggling like hell until the final shiver.

How many goddam guys, Matti was wondering, had it taken to manhandle Danny the Ape that way?

For the first time in a long time, the chief of the "elite" Wolf Crew was shaken and worried over the outcome of an assignment. He moved quickly to the

40

corner of the building and passed a sign to Vasquez, who hurriedly joined him there.

Matti informed the wheelman, "Someone noosed Danny and threw him off the roof. The other Ape's still in there—alive or dead I don't know. Tell Bill we go up and bring him out. Get the car ready, we're scrubbing this goddam thing."

Vasquez jerked his head in understanding and ran softly to the rear to pass the word to Wild Bill Stewart, then he retired to his position with the vehicle.

Matti and Stewart were barely into the building when a woman came through the rear exit. She wore a pants-suit and carried a suitcase. A scarf or something covered her head, looping down into a loose knot beneath the chin.

The wheelman could not get a good look at her—and he was not particularly interested. Wild Bill must have seen her, and he would not have let her by if she hadn't been okay.

The woman stepped into a car at the rear and eased it toward the far back corner of the building.

Something dropped to the ground back there, in the shadows beside the car. A door quickly opened and closed, and the vehicle went on around without so much as a pause in its forward motion.

Vasquez fidgeted for a moment of agonized indecision, then he jumped into the crew wagon and leaned on the horn.

Both Matti and Stewart erupted from the rear exit seconds later and the wheelman picked them up there.

"What is it?" Matti panted.

"A broad came out," Vasquez reported, the words tumbling together. "Bill must've bumped her going in, so I didn't pay much attention first. Carrying a bag, got into this Porsche was parked back here. Down there at the corner this guy dropped in from somewhere. Hell I almost didn't even see him. They split, fast."

Stewart said, "I didn't see no broad."

Buck the Ape came pounding around from the front of the building and leapt into the rear seat with Wild Bill Stewart, gasping his breathless report as he did so. "A guy went down the outside from the roof! Jumped into this sports car! Headed downtown!"

Vasquez had the vehicle rolling. Tensely, he asked, "What about Danny?"

"Stop up front," Matti growled.

They delayed long enough in the upper drive to pick up the remains of their fallen comrade, which they unceremoniously stuffed into the trunk compartment, then the Wolf Crew minus one was off and running in a hot pursuit.

"Just one guy?" Matti asked Buckholzer, as though nothing had transpired since that gasping report.

"That's all I saw, and I didn't really *see* him. Just a shadow moving down the building. The son of a bitch shinned right down that brick wall, drain pipe or something, five fucking floors."

"Must've been more," Matti argued. "No one guy could've done that to Danny, not that quick'n easy."

"I don't know," the wheelman said in a thoughtful

tone. "Like Buck, all I saw was this shadow-like something. Bet your ass, though, it wasn't more than one guy. If it *was* a guy."

"What're you thinking?" the crew-chief prompted him. All of the Wolf Crew respected the opinion and "feels" of the Bandalero.

Vasquez remained silent until he had the vehicle smoothly tracking in pursuit of the distant taillights, then he replied, "I think it was a guy, sure. And I think he was wearing black clothes, I mean total black . . . like he meant to be hard to spot in the dark. We saw what he done to Danny the Ape. I think. . . ."

Matti said, "Yeah .. ?" in the tone of a man who had already answered his own query.

"Bolan!" Buckholzer exclaimed in a church whisper.

"That's what I think," Vasquez agreed.

"Aw shit," Wild Bill Stewart protested, "that bastard's up in Bean City."

"*Was*," the crewchief growled. "He hasn't been seen or heard from for nearly a week."

"I think he's been heard from now," Vasquez muttered.

"Don't lose sight of that car!" Matti commanded.

"Don't worry, I got 'im. I told you, a Porsche. They got lights like nothing else on the road."

"I want the guy," Buckholzer announced coldly. "I got the right, I want him."

Matti said, "Knock it off, Buck. Danny was special to all of us, but you know the rule on vendettas. We run this outfit on *head*, not heart."

43

"Just the same, he belongs to me," the ex-AP insisted.

"That broad," Vasquez mused, probably trying to head off a showdown of authority. "Isn't she from up around Bean City somewhere?"

"Yeah," Matti growled. "Her old man was with the Boston mob when he got hit."

"Was that Smilin' Jack Vitale?" Stewart asked.

"That was him," the crewchief confirmed.

"So there's your tie," Vasquez said. He grunted as the car lights ahead swept into a diagonal crossroad. "Okay, they took Virginia Avenue. Now watch me head 'em off at the pass." He swung the car into a hard ninety-degree turn at the next intersection and powered along on a tangential pursuit of the other vehicle's track.

Matti warned, "Don't get so cute you lose 'em."

The wheelman brushed aside the caution, picking up again on his earlier line of thought. "That's the tie. The broad's from Boston, Bolan was last seen in Boston. He got onto her up there. That's him, all right. I can taste the bastard. That's him."

Half-humorously, Wild Bill Stewart declared, "I don't know if I want to laugh or cry about that."

"We might," Matti commented grimly, "want to be doing a little bit of both before this night is over."

"You take care of the crying, then," Buckholzer said. "I'll take care of the laughing."

"You watch your smart ass," the crewchief said ominously. "This is no time to be dicking around with a lot of emotional horseshit."

44

"I want the bastard, Frank," Buckholzer replied. His tone was somewhat subdued but still adamant. "Just don't get in my way. I want his fucking head."

Vasquez again moved smoothly in to avert a showdown. "What about the assignment?" he said, as though just remembering the original mission. "What d'we do about that Spinella hit?"

Matti growled, "Buck told me something had been slaughtered in the broad's bathroom. I guess Bolan beat us to it."

Bill Stewart chuckled and commented, "I guess we owe the bastard a favor."

"I guess the broad feels the same way," Matti said.

"Cut out the shit," Buckholzer said solemnly. "Let's decide this while we got time. I want his head."

Matti and Vasquez exchanged quick glances. Matti sighed and braced himself as the pursuit car swerved into another hair-raising turn. "Okay, Buck," he said, resigning from the contest of will. "His fucking head is all yours."

"You just watch what I do with it," Buckholzer replied.

A moment of silence later the wheelman tensely announced, "Okay, I'm on them. Get ready."

"Run 'em into the damn Capitol!" Matti commanded.

"Say the word," Vasquez replied, "and I'll run them right *up* the fucking thing."

The snout of Matti's submachine gun slid into the window opening. "Just get me ten feet closer," he commanded.

"Remember he's mine," the surviving Ape warned, breathing hard in anticipation of the kill. "Just slow 'im down for me."

"Okay, okay!" Matti growled. "But you better be as good as you think you are, buddy."

"Watch me," Buckholzer suggested, unsheathing his .45 Colt. "And watch what I do with Bolan's head."

Frank Matti really was not worried in the least about Buck the Ape's combat capabilities. But ... Mack Bolan was something else again. Yeah. That bastard was going to be no easy hit.

Less than a car-length now separated the two speeding vehicles. "Goddammit," Matti barked to the wheelman. "Get me alongside."

3: CAPITOL HIT

Claudia Vitale was aware of the pursuit from the moment the chase vehicle careened out of the parking lot, far to the rear. The grimfaced man beside her had also been watching for it, and he told her, "Cute, but not cute enough. They're on us."

The traffic was appallingly light. Only three sets of headlamps were running between the two vehicles.

"This is a honey of a car," Claudia murmured tensely. "I think we can outrun them."

"No way," the big guy said. "Let's not add cops to the chase. Did you recognize any of those people?"

She shook her head. "I've heard talk about an elite goon squad, though, reporting directly to Lupo. And there's supposed to be five of them."

"There's only four now," he muttered.

"Did you. . . ?"

The icy-quiet voice replied, "One of them found me."

Claudia shivered with the simplicity of that cold pronouncement. This was a man she had never known before; she had known many.

47

"What do we do?" she asked him.

"Keep running," he replied softly. "Until we want them to catch up."

She shivered again. "You're actually going to confront them?"

"No other way," he told her. "Once these people get on your tail, there's only one way to get them off."

She was keeping a check on the progress of the chase via the rearview mirror. "They're getting pretty close," she commented.

"Turn southeast onto Virginia," he instructed. "Then east on Constitution. Get me some place with some combat stretch."

"Some place with what?"

"A park, an open area with no people, anything like that."

At that time of night, in that town, it was an easy request. She made the turn onto Virginia Avenue and watched with a fluttering heart as the headlamps following swerved in behind them, then whipped across into another angular street and off the track.

Immediately the big grim man beside her snapped, "Okay, they're reading us! Pull over!"

She applied the brakes and pulled to the curb without comment, following Bolan's instructions when he commanded, "Hit the floor! Make yourself as small as possible and don't even breathe hard!"

Something beyond her comprehension was coming up, she realized that. It was a game for experts, as incomprehensible as football and all the talk about "reading the defense" and "reading the offense." She knew something very angry was about to happen, and she was entirely willing and grateful to have an expert calling the signals for her side.

Bolan slid over, took the wheel and sent the vehicle into whining traction along the same track, then he pulled another weapon from beneath the seat and lay it on his lap. It was a big, impressive, silver pistol—fully a foot long—of the type which feeds bullets from a clip in the handle.

"Listen to me," he was telling her. "When I say *go,* that means you. You bail out, hit the ground crawling like hell and don't look back. You get clear and you stay clear until you hear me calling you back. Understand?"

Claudia understood. She also knew instinctively that this cool warrior was making this particular fight on her behalf, serving up his own life in the defense of hers. She felt unworthy, tarnished, certainly undeserving of such a champion.

One did not, however, question the hand of providence. Claudia Vitale had unquestioningly accepted the protection of Mack Bolan, until very recently her gravest enemy.

"Good luck," she whispered from the floor of the speeding vehicle. And she meant it, with all her heart.

The Porsche was speeding into the vehicular loop of Capitol Hill, handling much better in those sweeping curves than the big crew-wagon, and wheelman Vasquez was having a tough time jockeying in for the kill. To make matters worse, the Porsche was hugging the inside curb, leaving the centrifugal handicap to the chase car.

Even for the Capitol grounds it was that time of night when they had the place all to themselves; not another vehicle was in sight and the track was almost as good as the Indy 500.

As the two cars roared toward the straightaway fronting the big domed building, Matti yelled, "Goddammit, get me alongside!"

"Hang on," the wheelman warned, giving the big car a reckless surge forward.

At that precise moment, the Porsche drifted out across their path in a plunge toward the outside.

Matti screamed, *"Look-out!"*

Vasquez was already reacting, instinctively following the drift with his own wheel.

The bastard in the Porsche, he realized, was a hell of a wheelman himself. It had been a planned maneuver and the sports car held all the advantage in this sort of road game. The Porsche whipped back toward the center but Vasquez was too far gone to recover.

They hit the outside curbing with the left-front wheel and bounded over in a wild plunge. The wheelman thought he had lost it for sure, and he was bracing for a roll. But the heavy vehicle held its wheels and plowed on into the trees lining the drive.

To his dying day Vasquez would never be able to explain how he managed to avoid a head-on into one of those trees. They sideswiped several as he fought the vehicle to a metal-grinding halt—Matti cussing a blue streak all the while and trying to shove his feet through the floorboards, the gunners in the rear grunting and damning the wild bronco ride and flopping about like a couple of buoys in troubled water.

And when the wild plunge was ended, matters immediately became much worse.

The Porsche had arced about into a U-turn and was already parked.

Vasquez could see the big guy in black charging out of there with a gun in each hand and running straight for them.

Matti had the door on his side open and the chopper already spitting flame as he struggled to the outside.

Vasquez kicked his door open and tumbled to the ground, dragging the sawed-off shotgun with him.

Okay, he was thinking, *you wanted him, Buck. So goddammit take him, what're you waiting for?*

He heard the boom of a big handgun as Matti's Thompson began drawing return fire, then another and another—and Vasquez actually *heard* the bullet that connected with the crewchief. The Thompson crashed across the hood of the car and tumbled to the ground. Matti toppled over the other way, holding his belly and shrieking something in a voice which was fast losing steam.

The big handgun was raising hell in rapid fire now, and bullets like cannonballs were thudding into the vehicle.

Wild Bill Stewart came staggering out of the rear

51

door on the wheelman's side, fighting to get his Thompson into the battle while taking cover behind the vehicle.

Buckholzer stepped out of the other side with blood spurting from his neck, not even a gun showing.

Vasquez raised to a knee, and across the few feet of hell-ground the two "elite" hitmen locked gazes for a frozen moment, then another sizzling projectile crunched into Buck's skull and it went to pieces in a spraying shower, some of it splattering across the car and onto the wheelman.

Vasquez suddenly felt very sick, and he crawled away from there as the stuttering reports of Wild Bill's automatic were interspersed with the continuing big booms of the silver handgun. Then the stuttering stopped.

He threw one last look across his shoulder as he got to his feet and ran out of hell, and the scene back there was one which would remain with him forever.

The big guy in black—Bolan, for damned sure—just standing there with those two guns filling his hands. The shattered crew wagon. Buck and Wild Bill and Gung-ho Matti reduced to unmoving lumps of elite nothingness. The lighted dome of the Capitol backdropping and adding to the macabre quality of the thing. Capitol cops erupting and spilling down the steps.

And Bandalero Vasquez felt no guilt whatever at quitting that place on the run.

The guy, Bolan, was as big as his reputation, that was for sure. And now he was in Washington.

The important thing now was to get the word to Lupo. And that might not be the easiest task in the world to accomplish. The guy was harder to find than Whistler's father, what with all the security razzmatazz.

He for damn sure had to be told, one way or another. Bolan had a way of turning everything upside down, of spitting in the face of odds and coming through smelling like a rose.

So, sure ... the important thing now was to get to Lupo and tell him. The game had changed. The Wolf had to be told that the Tiger had come to town.

Despite himself, Vasquez had to smile in grudging admiration of the bastard. What a hit—what a *hell* of a hit that had been.

But the guy had gone too far, now. He had endorsed his own death certificate. That much was certain.

Nobody had ever taken on Lupo and lived to brag about it.

Neither would Mack Bolan.

The son of a bitch was as good as dead.

4: THE PROBLEM

Bolan had not come to Washington to rescue maidens in distress nor to engage enemy gun crews in pointless firefights. Sometimes, though, a guy found himself in a pure-reaction situation—and such was the case with Claudia Vitale.

He'd stumbled across Claudia's tracks while gathering intelligence against a wheeler-dealer known by the code name of "Al 88" during the Boston battle. And he'd understood immediately that some ominous intrigues were afoot in the nation's capitol.

A full-blown mob conspiracy against the nation's governmental machinery was practically verified by a U.S. Justice Department official, Harold Brognola, an old "friend" who fed Bolan's intelligence into the central crime computer at Washington.

Brognola, a grudging and often unwilling "accomplice" to the Bolan campaigns, was thoroughly shaken by the implications that organized crime had strongly infiltrated the congress, the federal judiciary, and various executive departments of official Washington. There were even indications that high levels of the justice department were involved in the take-over, and the shaken official was distrustful of his own superiors. It was Brognola's suggestion that "a touch of Bolan" might be needed to clear the Washington atmosphere. It was not an official invitation, of course —nor even a personal one. Mack Bolan was on the FBI's "most wanted" list. He was sought by the police of a dozen states and of several sovereign nations.

The long relationship with Harold Brognola had run an erratic course. At one time the justice department official had quietly maneuvered for secret governmental sanctions of the Executioner crusades, seeing in Bolan the most formidable weapon ever to arise in the war on organized crime.

Bolan had refused the "secret portfolio" of official backing.

"I don't want a license to kill," he explained.

He would conduct his own war his own way and he would meet "the final judgment of the universe" standing on his own two feet.

Later developments had borne out the wisdom of that decision.

As his war escalated and expanded, official pressures became intense and Brognola was eventually given personal responsibility for the government's "stop Bolan" counter-war. He had very nearly fulfilled that responsibility during the battle for Las Vegas.

In the aftermath of that experience, Brognola had confided to Leo Turrin, another Bolan "ally": "Hell, I couldn't do it, Leo. I just couldn't gun the guy down in cold blood. From a distance, maybe I could ...

even in the back. But I couldn't look that man in the eye and shoot him. Not *that* guy."

A curious fact of the Bolan wars was that despite the man's desperate situation and his many close scrapes with entrapment, he had never once been known to fire upon a police officer.

Entries in his personal journal repeatedly reflected his feelings in this regard. At Pittsfield, for example:

"The cops are just doing their job. I can't fight them, I simply have to avoid them."

And a short while later, in Los Angeles:

"I'm not above the law. In the final analysis, justice under law is the only hope for mankind. But sometimes a man just can't go by the book. I can't turn away from this fight simply because it conflicts with certain ideals. There is a higher ideal at work here. At the same time, I have to keep my respect for the law. We are working toward the same end."

During a run through Arizona, he recorded this cancellation of a planned strike:

"Just in time, Leo says an undercover man is inside this operation. No way to tip him. Mission scrubbed."

A San Francisco note about cops had this to say:

"They are soldiers of the same side."

Perhaps the most revealing of all is this message to himself during the Manhattan wars:

"I have a rage to survive, I know that. The animal in a man dies hard. I have to keep con-

56

ditioning myself to accept death from a cop,
when it finally comes down to that."

It was a tightrope which Bolan was walking, a
precarious balance between the law and the lawless,
and he was forever in danger of being ripped apart
by either side.

Although many lawmen respected the Executioner
in the same sense that he respected them, others did
not find it so easy to manipulate their sense of duty.
Still others saw the blitzing warrior as a genuine
menace to society and some regarded him as only a
feather to be added to their cap of personal ambition.

In the final picture, the entire world was a jungle
of survival for this very able jungle fighter, and his
decision to "go it alone" was probably dictated by a
highly sensitized survival instinct.

Even his contacts with Leo Turrin, the undercover
cop at Pittsfield and Bolan's closest friend, were conducted with the utmost caution. Anyone, at any time,
for a variety of reasons, could suddenly become "the
enemy." Like a jungle cat, Mack Bolan trusted no
man implicitly and looked warily at every proffered
hand of friendship.

So the Executioner certainly had not come to
Washington in response to an official invitation, as
rumored, nor had he been "nudged there" by Harold
Brognola, as the latter perhaps had reason to believe.

Actually Bolan had already committed himself to a
probe of the Washington atmosphere before listening
to Brognola's misgivings concerning "high level
treachery."

He had come because of his own deep feelings that something was terribly rotten in the nation's capitol, and because all the signs pointed toward a "big happening" in the very near future.

And he told Claudia Vitale, shortly after the Capitol Hill firefight: "Stop apologizing. I saved you for selfish reasons. I'm here to sabotage the master timetable in any way I can. If you want to square yourself with your conscience, now's your chance. Otherwise goodbye and go to hell. I don't want any cute games, lady, and I haven't time for romantic intrigues. So declare yourself here and now. I've got to get this show on the road."

Claudia "declared" herself, and the intelligence which she ripped off in thirty breathless minutes was enough to convince the Executioner that he had stumbled into ripe grounds indeed.

She also told him, "It's the old game done up in bright new costumes. Ward politics in all their viciousness, elevated to a national scale. Threats, violence, blackmail, intimidation of every stripe and directed at every seat in congress, every staff, every bureaucratic office. They're rewriting the laws of the nation and doing it so cleverly that no single victim on Capitol Hill is even aware of what's really happening. New bills are being watered down in committee or else totally mutilated in order to favor criminal interests—and their interests range into almost everything now. Some bills are even being drafted by syndicate lawyers and slipped into the mill by their connections. Anyone they can't buy or intimidate is disposed of—one way or another. They can kill their character reputation, their political careers, or they can smash their bodies—and they're doing it all. That's what finally turned me away. Those envelopes you saw me delivering ... they weren't payoffs. Those were threats, evidence for blackmail, that sort of thing. I haven't made a cash payoff since Lupo made the scene. He doesn't believe in buying what he already owns."

So ... yes ... the battle lines were firmly drawn. Bolan did not know, the entire enemy, but he knew what they were doing, how and why.

The next move was his.

He had to disrupt a zero-hour countdown for domination of a nation's governmental functions. It seemed almost silly even to contemplate such a take-over—in a country as powerful and progressive as the United States—but if it wasn't a silly idea to the mob, then neither was it silly to Mack Bolan.

He had to ferret out the dry-rot in the national capital's institutions, expose those who were unfit to serve, protect all he could those who had simply been sucked into an operation too powerful to fight.

He had to stop the mob at every turn, at every reach, at every attempted movement toward control in Washington ... and he had to run their rotten asses out of there.

Could one man do all that?

Yes. One man could do a hell of a lot. If he was totally committed to his goals. If he could harden his guts—his very soul—to wade through rivers of blood and never look back. If he had the tools, the energies, the talents and if he would apply them all unsparingly.

Mack Bolan was such a man.

Yes. He could do all that.

But only if the gods were willing.

5: THE RECORD

From an entry in Mack Bolan's personal journal ...

Washington, 18 April

At a time like this I regret my lack of formal education. There are things I want to record here—feelings, mostly—and that can be a tough job for a guy who has spent his lifetime soldiering.

This may be my last chance to get it into the record, to try to explain why I sent my life along the course it is now on.

I try to tell myself that I don't mind being called a murdering lunatic ... but I do, I mind. No man who is sane enjoys being pointed out as an enemy of his society. I guess what I mind the most, though, is that so damned much official attention is going to my side of the war and not to the other.

It's a lot like the Vietnam problem. All the noise and agonizing over the morality of the thing, with no really close look at the reasons for it. You can't make a problem like that go away by simply debating the right or wrong of it. Both sides to any debate are usually sincere. What bothers me is when one side seizes the "morality" stick—as though there is always but one morality and everything else must kneel to it.

That makes it pretty easy for some people. It isn't too hard to cop out when you have "morality" on your side.

I didn't really want this war with the Mafia. I sort of edged into it, the way our government did in Vietnam. Once in, though, there's nothing left but to see the thing through, for better or worse. I couldn't run from the mob now. That would give them a strength they'd never had before. It would wipe out every advance I've made, and it would actually make things worse than when this war started.

I did not want to come to Washington. Everything inside of me kept telling me to bypass this town, to take an R & R or to try a softer spot.

What the hell, my army is worn thin. Barefoot, tattered, reserves just about exhausted. I'm in no shape to be storming the national bastion.

But, hell, I had to check into this one. I didn't bring it here, it was already here. And it looks like it's for all the marbles. How could I bypass it?

I have this feeling that the entire focus of my life has become fixed on this spot; that I will very likely die here. If that's the way it has to be, then okay. I've known all along that there was only one way out of this mess for me. What I mind is failing, and failing at such a hell of a critical time. Also, I don't feel that the mob will put me down. I believe it will be the law, and I'm afraid that the focus will go the wrong way. Big deal, they got Mack Bolan. Never mind the marauding cannibals who were left around to pick up the pieces. That's what bothers me.

I'm no politician and I am not talking politics when I say that my present war is no more than an extension (or maybe it's a contraction) of that other war in Vietnam. I never did have the feeling that I was fighting to save the world from Communism or for any political ideals. I fought, the best way I knew how, simply because I felt the call to battle. It was a personal war for me, the same as this one is.

It's a war of principle.

I can't really do anything about Vietnam. But *this* country, and the real problems we face here is something I can tackle.

And I'm worried about the outcome of this Washington battle.

Ten years ago I wouldn't have been so worried. We were a different nation then. I guess what scares me is the sinking feeling that the country has lost its guts. Everyone seems to be hung up on ideas of doing their own thing, living in peace and sweetness and love. Hell I can't blame anyone for wanting that. I want it too, not this hell I'm stuck with now. All those nice things, though, come with a price tag. *Some* one has to be willing to settle the bill, or there will be no seller and no buyer.

I've never had any illusions that I am saving the country, or that I am even going about things the right way. I only know that it is *my* way. I can't even think in terms of right and wrong. I'm simply doing what I have to do, and I don't care if anyone understands or not. I know, even, that my way will never make much of a dent in the mob. They'll walk over my mangled body one of these days soon, my "delaying action" will be finished, and the world will not even remember my name. To hell with "glory," I'm not looking for that.

None of that is to the point.

The point is that this country had better get its head together damned soon or the mob will be walking over *its* mangled body.

I keep getting back to the Vietnam thing, in my mind, but that's because it is all so interconnected. I wouldn't want to go back to 'Nam—no man in his right mind would. But if it were not for this new war, I know I'd be going back. I'd have to, for my own peace of mind. Cannibalism is a disease. It spreads when unopposed. Go ask the Mafia. If a national attitude of "peace at any price" carries over into this closer cannibalism at home, then I feel nothing but doubly dead in a very troubled grave.

Sometimes, dammit, you've got to be ready to sacrifice peace in favor of a higher morality ... and don't anyone think that peace itself is the highest order of things.

It can be the lowest order.

Peace, in its ultimate form, is death.

I'm expounding like an expert with a Ph.D. in Life, I know, but it doesn't take a degree to recognize the truth when you're staring right into it.

I have stared into a lot of raw truth these past few months.

Life is violence, motion, a striving, a non-peace, a fighting for the good and a determination to go on functioning.

Maybe I should be classified as one of the cannibals myself. I prefer to think of myself as a counter-cannibal. I can't see much value to a livingness built entirely of peace and love and sweetness—not when you are turning away from life itself. When you live with constant death, you begin to see what life is really all about.

I do know that the traditional idea of "heaven" seems silly to me. I could not live in a silly heaven. Most people I've ever known could not. They'd run screaming into hell long before the seventh day. I'm wandering afield here, but I have to get this down also. Most of the people I have known who yearn so for the eternity of heaven can hardly stand one hour a week in church. How the hell are they going to remain sane through an everlasting round of hosannas?

The guy who designed and built this awesome universe would also go nuts in that kind of "heaven." He's a do-er, a mover, a builder—not a psalm-singer.

I guess this all does figure in. I'm getting my head together, I guess. What I'm trying to say is simply this. Life itself is a violence. Living, when it's worthwhile, is a conflict. It's a reach toward total agitation, not total rest. Take away the conflict, take away the goals and the struggle for them, and friend you are living in some sort of silly heaven.

Total agitation is simply another way of saying "violence." Life itself is a consummation of violence. We all kill and ingest other living things so that we may go on living. Even the gentle doe mangles and crushes and digests the beautifully-alive wild flowers, adding them to her own storehouse of life, and she does so without a quiver of conscience. This is the universal nature of life.

The human mind knows that there are unacceptable limits of violence, though. Maybe that's what this process of human evolution is all about, maybe it's the universe growing a conscience. A civilized man understands that this violence of lifeform upon lifeform must be controlled and restricted as much as possible.

The trouble is, some men never become civilized.

They respond to only one thing—counterviolence, or at least the promise of it.

That is why peace marches are so damned futile.

You can't unilateral yourself out of a cannibal's pot.

Someone has to keep the cannibals in line ... with a big stick.

Okay, that's what I'm doing in Washington. And I guess it's also why I'm so damned worried about dying here. The job is not finished, not even nearly. The cops can't handle the thing without the help of an aroused people, and nobody around here seems to be alarmed about anything except the war in Vietnam.

I'd like to see some *war* marches in this country.

The mob is eating you alive, people. Right now they've only reached to about your shinbone. Pretty soon, though, they'll be eating your heads, and you'll damn sure be alarmed then.

6: MARKED

Carlo Spinella was a newly made underboss under the equally new *Capo* Gus Riappi, the latter being successor to the late Arnesto (Arnie the Farmer) Castiglione who was gunned down by Bolan during the British campaign.

According to the best intelligence readings, the crown of domain had not yet firmly settled onto Riappi's ambitious head but the coronation seemed a foregone conclusion, especially since Bolan had also recently eliminated Tony Lavagni, the only competitor in the field.

Spinella himself had been strictly a neighborhood-level boss, running various rackets in and around the national capital under the sponsorship of Big Gus. He had never had jurisdiction in political/governmental circles, however. His specialty items were girls, drugs, numbers, vending machines, a payday loan racket and several bookie joints. He was also a silent partner in two bars, a pool hall and a real estate enterprise consisting of ownership of two blocks of rundown dwellings in Washington's most blighted ghetto section.

The Spinella "crew" was relatively small. At the moment of Bolan's entry into the Washington scene, the "Southwest Boss" had ten soldiers in his official cadre who functioned primarily as enforcers and "controllers," bossing a larger army of blacks who actually ran the rackets. In addition to these ten, he had four "house men" who saw to the physical protection of his body. These fourteen constituted the entire Spinella "crew." Bolan had removed three of these from the scene at the first point of contact.

With Tony Lavagni dead and Big Gus elevated to the exalted status of *Capo* of the lower-Atlantic seaboard, the small-spuds Spinella had seen nothing but roses in his personal future. By all that was right and holy, he would emerge from the shuffle as the official boss of the entire District of Columbia.

Myopia had quickly settled into that rosy view, however.

Big Gus had been sent down to the Caribbean to help Lavagni trap Bolan, on orders from the Old Men themselves. Lavagni came back in a casket or his surviving pieces did. Big Gus himself came slinking back in disgrace, his tail between his legs—licking his bruised ego with a vengeance.

Carlo Spinella had suffered that vengeance.

Big Gus took over all of the old Lavagni territory, his holdings, accounts, and crew—everything.

The son of a bitch was just taking while the taking was good. Carlo knew that.

Maybe, just maybe, the *Commissione* would figure that any guy who couldn't handle a simple job like the Caribbean hit wasn't fit to wear the crown of the entire lower Atlantic seaboard.

So Big Gus Riappi was taking what he could while he could.

What the hell, Riappi was Spinella's boss. Come hell or high water, disgrace or whatever, that was the way things were.

Even after the official blessings and forgiveness had come down from the Old Men, even when Big Gus knew damned well that he had the whole damned Castiglione empire in his pocket—even then he'd continued to exercise direct control of the Washington territory.

Boss or no boss, that wasn't right. It wasn't justice, not for a loyal underboss like Carlo Spinella.

Things like that rankled a guy. They burned at his guts and woke him up in the middle of the night, they even got him to talking to himself and mistreating his own people.

The thing, of course, that was making Big Gus behave this way was that damnable Lupo.

Jesus! but Carlo hated that guy.

The new wave, they called heads like Lupo. The new wave of well educated, smooth talking society hoods who'd never been down in the ranks, never down on the streets, ninety-day-wonders who moved in on the top and never knew what it was to pull a territory together from nothing and make the goddam thing *hum.*

70

Nationals.

Carlo hated nationals.

But it was the new wave, yeah. A guy couldn't fight it, not even a guy like Big Gus Riappi could fight it. The older bosses, sure—what the hell, they *were* the nationals, the *commissione*. The Old Men didn't have to worry about heads like Lupo. Hell, they'd *created* them.

Fucking fancypants bastards with their college educations.

Big Gus hated Lupo as much as Carlo did.

And with better reasons.

The Old Men had decided that Washington should be declared an open city. But Carlo knew—they had made that decision so they could send Lupo in there. If that wasn't an invasion of holy territory then just what the hell was it.

Nobody—not Carlo Spinella, not Big Gus, not *nobody* in the whole damn Washington area—nobody could lay a hand on Lupo.

The son of a bitch had a license, he had a commission directly from the Old Men, and Big Gus had been ordered to cooperate with him "in every way possible."

If Lupo said "cool the action for a few days"—then they had to cool the action. It might interfere with something "delicate" Lupo was trying to work. Meanwhile, money was being lost. Lost money never got recovered, Carlo had learned well that grim fact of life. It was like a piece of ass—every piece missed

71

was a piece gone forever—there was no way of catching up.

And if Lupo said "send me over a gun crew"—then they had to send him over a gun crew. Something "delicate" had gone sour and turned into something brutal. But who paid the gunners, and who had to take care of their protection—who had to answer to the cops if a hit went sour? Not Lupo, *hell no*.

That guy had the whole District right under his thumb.

Yeah. Carlo hated the guy.

Probably, though, Big Gus hated him worse. More was at stake for Gus.

At this particular moment, however, it was a toss-up over which of them had a right to hate Lupo the most.

Via some twenty-five miles of telephone wire, Spinella was telling Riappi, "That's what I said, Gus. All three of them. Horse and Tommy and Chick—parked out in front of the house here. Dead as hell. It was that damn Wolf Crew, I know it was. They didn't even have the common decency to dump the bodies somewhere else, they left them right out here in front of my house. And they didn't even ring the bell or call or anything else. We didn't even find them first. The damn law got to them first, Gus. Now what the hell, is that adding insult to injury or isn't it? What the hell do I tell the law now?"

"Your boys carry credentials, don't they?" Riappi growled back.

"Sure, but what ice does that cut? Dead is dead, I gotta have a story for the law."

Riappi sighed as he replied, "You tell them no story, Carlo. Because you know nothing about it. It's as easy as that. Your boys are bonafide security agents in your south-west apartments. They probably made some enemies, that's all. They're victims of a black vendetta. You know the routine."

Following a tense silence, Spinella said, "Well that's not what's really bothering me, Gus. We can't let that guy get away with this kind of shit. We'll lose the respect of our own boys."

Riappi sounded regretful and conciliatory as he replied, "That was your fault, Carlo. I hate to say it but it's true. You started it, the whole thing, and what you did was wrong. You were fucking around with something way over your head, *fidele* ... we all would have been in hard trouble if you'd been allowed to go through with it. The way it is now, Lupo and me both are covering the thing. We're covering it for *you*, Carlo. We're sorry your boys had to pay the price. But that's the way it is sometimes, Carlo. When a guy fucks up as bad as you fucked—"

"I know, I know," Spinella agreed worriedly. "I still say Lupo should've let *us* in on his big secret. Well okay. If you say so, okay. I'm not bitching about anything I guess except the way they left my boys here without even saying hello about it. I mean, parking 'em dead right in front of my house. I take that as a warning, Gus, a very clear warning to *me*. I

73

think I should have gotten above that kind of thing. You know."

"Sure, I know," Riappi agreed. "Look, just cool it. Lupo's time will come, don't worry. He's running high, wide and handsome right now but he's building a lot of enemies while he's doing it. We'll all remember Lupo's sins, don't worry."

"He didn't have to *kill* those boys, Gus."

"Maybe he didn't and maybe he did. You should know your own boys better than I do. What do you think?"

Spinella snorted as he replied, "Maybe he did. I still don't think any broad in the world is worth three of my boys."

"This broad is, believe it and forget it," Riappi said quietly.

"I'll believe it but I won't forget it."

"Forget it, Carlo. For now."

"Okay. It's forgotten."

"Tell the cops what I told you. And don't worry. I already got the fix in."

"Oh, swell, I'm glad to hear that."

"No big wake for your boys, Carlo. Quiet, very quiet. And see you don't go yammering around about how they died. You know."

"Oh sure, hell, I know."

Riappi clicked off and Spinella slowly cradled the telephone, glaring at it as though it were something foul and slimy.

Which one, he was wondering, did he hate the most now? Lupo or Slimy Gus?

He slid off the bed and struggled into a robe, belting it tightly around silken pajamas, then he strode out to the "crew room"—a lounge area for his retinue of personal bodyguards.

Only Rocky Lucindo, the soldier who had brought the disturbing news to his bedside, was present—and he was standing tensely at the window and staring down onto the scene of confusion just below that window.

A couple of meat wagons were out there, several marked police cars, as well, and probably one or two unmarked official vehicles. Photographers were milling about and popping flashbulbs, some of the lenses being directed at the house itself. The street was blocked off to traffic, the cops trying to disperse a growing crowd of spectators. People in bathrobes ... broads with their hair up in curlers ... it was still pretty early in the day.

Lucindo was the chief houseman. He was an old soldier who went way back with Carlo Spinella. He was a close personal friend, perhaps the only man in the world whom Carlo trusted implicitly.

The triggerman muttered, "It's a circus out there. Why does everybody always want to see it?"

"Makes 'em feel good it's not them," Spinella replied caustically. He moved away from the window as another flashbulb pushed back the early-morning gloom. "What time is it?"

"About five," the bodyguard reported. "What did Big Gus have to say?"

"Same old crap. Cool it for now. Play dead." The

75

capo-regime snorted. "I'd like to cool you-know-who for now and forever."

"Just say the word," Lucindo replied soberly.

"Naw. We play it straight, just like Gus says. He's the boss. Where's Fred?"

Lucindo jerked his head toward the window. "Out there, with Ripper. Being concerned citizens. Ripper was the first one out there. He says those other soldiers are a mess, a hell of a mess. Gave it to them in the head, all of them."

Spinella shuddered and went to the bar. He poured a cup of coffee and carried it to the television, turned the set on, selected a channel, and eased onto an ottoman as he sipped the coffee and stared at the blank screen.

A moment later he growled, "Hell, is it that early?"

"I said five," the bodyguard reminded him. "Try that independent station, that channel uh. ..."

The hallway door opened and another man shoved head and shoulders through. "Plainclothes guy wants in," he reported. "Says it's just a routine—"

"Tell him," Lucindo snapped, "nobody saw nothing."

"Yeah but he wants to talk to Mr. Spinella."

"Tell him Mr. Spinella is too upset to see anybody right now. He'll give them a call when he's feeling better. What the hell, those cops got no feelings for the dead?"

The hardman replied with nothing but a tight smile and immediately withdrew.

The chief bodyguard went over to hover above his

boss. "What do we tell them, Carlo? We'll have to face it sooner or later."

"The niggers did it," Spinella replied quietly.

"Okay. I guess that's as good as anything."

"Sure. Lousy bastards never want to pay their rent. So they jumped our collectors. Probably robbed them. Then left the bodies at my front door just for kicks."

"One story is as good as another," Lucindo agreed.

The outer door opened again and the hardman reappeared, this time his face pulled into angry lines. "This guy has a John Doe warrant," he announced loudly.

Another man walked in behind him—a slightly built Negro of indeterminate age, sharply dressed, smiling soberly.

"Sorry to disturb you at this hour, Mr. Spinella," he said in a soft voice.

"So go disturb John Doe," Spinella growled, hardly looking up.

The smile remained. "We knew you'd be anxious to cooperate. That's a pretty brutal thing that happened to your boys."

"Employees," Spinella corrected him. "And you bet your ass I'll cooperate. If you don't have those people rounded up and behind bars by nightfall, I'll round 'em up myself."

"What people?" the cop asked.

"You know who I'm talking about, Walker. Those people of yours, those coloreds. They've been headed toward something like this for a year now."

The black detective knew it was a silly game; his

smile said so as he replied, "Maybe you're right. A lot of the younger men living in Rat Town are ex-GI's. Most of them infantry veterans of Vietnam. One of the latest equal job opportunities for those people of mine, those coloreds, fighting the nation's wars."

"So what?" Spinella asked in a muffled voice.

"So I guess some of them don't understand why they have to pay half their income to live in a squalor surpassing that of the Vietnamese. So ... maybe you're right, Mr. Spinella." The cop had produced a handkerchief from an inside pocket, and he was carefully unwrapping it. "I guess the ex-GI angle also explains this lone piece of physical evidence left behind by the killer. You ever see one of these things before? Careful now, don't touch."

He was holding the handkerchief directly under the *Mafioso's* nose. Spinella took one quick look at the metallic object revealed there. His eyes skittered away and his breath seemed to be clinging to his throat as he huskily asked, "Where'd you get that?"

"We found it on what was left of Tommy the Sandman's head," the black man explained.

Lucindo was craning over to get a look at the object, but the detective was already re-wrapping it and returning it to his pocket.

"Just wanted to ask," the cop was saying, "if the thing could have belonged to one of the victims. Ever see it before?"

Spinella's eyelids had dropped to about half-mast and he did not seem to be looking at anything in the physical world. "I seen a hundred of those things," he

78

replied mechanically. "You can buy 'em in any army store, nickle apiece. Now get outta here, Walker. Let me mourn my dead."

"Sure." The cop spun about and returned to the doorway. He hesitated there for a moment, then turned around for a parting shot. "I guess you're right, you can find these things anywhere. We found another one this morning, a few hours ago. Almost on the Capitol steps."

"Yeah?" The Mafia boss was not even attempting to conceal his interest.

"That's right. In the same place where we found four more murder victims. Male caucausians. One of them was one of *your* people, Mr. Spinella, one of those Italians."

"Who was it?" Spinella asked in a choking voice.

The cop shrugged. "Identification won't be positive until fingerprint verification comes in. But we believe he was Frank Matti."

Spinella's reaction was a mere flickering of the eyes. Detective Lieutenant Walker smiled again and went out, carefully closing the door behind him.

Lucindo strode halfway to the door in an almost explosive release of pent-up energy, then he whirled about and cried, "Matti and three of his boys! What the hell, Carlo?"

Spinella did not reply. He was staring at his fingers and softly tapping them against his thigh.

The two hardmen exchanged troubled glances and the one who had escorted the detective into the room blurted, "What'd he have in that handkerchief?"

"Hell I didn't get a look," Lucindo replied. He took a hesitant step toward his boss. "What was it, Carlo? What'd he show you?"

"One of them decorations," Spinella muttered. "Those shooting prizes. You know."

The chief bodyguard's voice was suddenly as deadened as the boss's as he said, "You mean marksman's medal."

"Yeah, I think that's what it was," Spinella growled.

"Oh God," Ripper quietly exclaimed.

Lucindo was frozen in his tracks, the body arched, a procession of emotions marching across the disturbed face.

Spinella was reaching for the telephone. "A death mark," he mumbled. "Left right at my front door."

"Who're you calling?" Lucindo wanted to know.

"Big Gus, who the hell you think. I'm not facing this alone. Bet your ass, Rocky, not *this* one."

"What's that goddam guy doin' in this town?" the bodyguard wondered aloud.

"I'll give you twenty guesses," Spinella replied sarcastically. He changed his mind about the phone and shoved it back. "*You* call," he instructed Lucindo. "Tell 'em what we know, and tell them to tell Gus I'm coming out." He heaved himself erect and headed for his bedroom. "I'm gonna shave and get dressed. We'll take the Lincoln. Get it ready."

Lucindo was already on the telephone and Ripper Aliotto was headed out the other door when Spinella passed into the bedroom.

He kicked the door shut and was peeling off the

80

robe when he became aware of a flicker of motion behind him, and before he could react the unmistakable pressure of a pistol's barrel was roughly applied to the back of his head.

A voice as cold as ice, yet hardly more than a whisper, advised him, "Easy, Carlo, and you might live awhile."

And that, Carlo wryly reflected, was the best offer he'd had all night.

7: THE UNDERSTANDING

The guy stood a full head taller than Spinella but he was probably no heavier. The two-hundred-odd pounds which were distributed along that stretched-out frame were all hard ones. You knew that by the way the guy stood poised there in an agile balancing of the muscular systems, by the cat-like movements and the spring-tension control which seemed to accompany his command of the enemy environment.

"I want no shitting around," the Executioner softly told the Mafia underboss, and the cold authority in that voice matched the rest of the man.

Carlo Spinella had no inclination whatever for shitting around.

He fought his tumbling emotions to a paralyzed standstill as he woodenly assured the intruder, "I got no hard feelings for you, Bolan."

Death was staring at him, *Death*, with a capital *D* and all edged with ice as it held command over those penetrating blue eyes. Spinella could not repress a trickling shiver.

He tried again. "We got nothing to argue about, Mack."

"I'm not your judge," Mr. Death quietly announced. "I didn't come to argue."

The guy shoved him onto the bed and a marksman's medal hit the soft surface at about the same moment, inches from Spinella's panicky eyes.

His very breath was hurting as it fought clear of constricted air passages. There was a roaring in his ears and he hurt all over, from head to toe, everywhere—even his hair hurt.

So this was what it was like, then. This was what it felt like to meet the end of everything a guy had planned for and worked for and sweated for throughout a harsh lifetime. This was the end of the trick—and there was pain, yes, real physical pain, in that realization.

In that one frozen moment all the dreams and agonies of a mis-spent lifetime floated free and spiraled into that peaking awareness of death, the memories of violence received and given, the regrets long buried and glossed over by successive layers of tantalizing ambitions, fleeting frames of broads laid and broads missed, of love offered and spurned and sometimes trampled—and agonies of the soul, too, very real agonies which now knew no possibility of atonement. A life in hock had come due, the note was being presented for payment in full and Carlo Spinella knew that he had come up bankrupt.

The guy was angling a black Beretta right into Carlo's face. It was ominously tipped with a long silencer, making it look twice as long as any gun had a right to be, and—yes, Carlo knew. He knew.

"You won't make it out of here, guy," he whispered. "No way, no chance. My boys are all over the joint. Cops running up and down the street outside. This's dumb, real dumb."

The big guy replied, "The mob pronounced me dead several lifetimes ago." He shrugged those muscled shoulders and added, "What does a dead man have to lose?"

Spinella's mouth was like packed with cotton and he felt that he was strangling on his own words as he said, "Okay, how do I beat it? Look, I'm not ready for this. There's just no sense to it, it's dumb to die this way. I don't even know you, we never even saw each other before. Why should we be doing this? Huh? What's the sense? Hey, God, Bolan, let's at least talk it over."

Surprisingly, unbelievably, the guy gave that frozen face about a one-millimeter tilt and he told the doomed man, "Okay. But no arguments, Carlo."

Hope was reborn.

A new mortgage, maybe, was being issued in the spiritual court of last resort. But it was a tenuous reprieve, obviously contingent entirely upon absolute honesty with no cuteness and no reservations.

He could, of course, yell like hell for the housemen. He might get, maybe, half a yell into the air before it was met by the sizzler from that silenced Beretta. And, yeah, the guy would then have a fight on his hands. He'd probably die right beside Carlo.

Small damn comfort.

Spinella reached eagerly for the note on his life.

"I'm done arguing," he muttered. "Listen, Bolan, you're right. It's a rotten outfit. They make a lot of noise about brotherhood and honor and all that crap, but it's just a lot of crap after all. Hey, they never gave me nothing, not a damn thing. They *allowed* me to operate, that's all. What I got, I got myself— and half of that I have to turn back to them. It's a big con job, Bolan. We just run around conning each other."

The big guy just said, "Yeah."

The speech obviously had more meaning to Spinella than to his audience. Mainly, he supposed, because he had actually faced the truth for the first time. It was almost blinding, that kind of truth. It was deathbed truth.

"I mean it," he whispered, with all the awe of a man who had suddenly known a mystical experience.

Bolan said, "Okay, show me. Go to the door. Open it one inch, no more. Call your house captain in here. Then get clear."

God! Call Rocky in to his death?

That was it, of course. It was the guy's only way out. Call them in one by one, knock them off one by one, then it would be Carlo's turn.

Bolan must have read the thoughts that were tumbling through that tortured mind. He told the *Mafioso*, "It's your only card, Carlo. Play it or cash out."

Spinella played it.

He got off the bed and staggered to the door,

85

paused a moment to stare about the room in confusion as he straightened his dressing gown, then he cracked the door open and called, "Hey, Rock. Getcher ass in here a minute."

He heard Rocky's responding growl and he retreated immediately, leaving the door slightly ajar, dropping tensely onto the edge of the bed and staring at the floor.

He did not want to see Rocky get it.

They had been friends, they were a long ways down the road together, but there was not even a feeling of guilt or treachery ... simply regret. At a time like this, a guy did not split the hairs of life ... he simply clung to them.

Lucindo barged in with his usual display of energy, banging the door behind him like the bull in the china closet he'd always been. Spinella loved that big gorilla, really loved him like the brother he'd never had. He could not look at him.

"Okay they're expecting us," the bodyguard announced. "Ripper's getting the car—"

He knew.

The breath just suddenly deserted his speech and he stared at Spinella's grudgingly upraised gaze—and, yeah, poor Rocky knew.

He cried, "Carlo, what the hell ..." and exploded into the final defensive move of his life, throwing himself sideways and clawing for the revolver in the shoulder-holster as he tried to spin into a confrontation with the big guy in the shadows.

An eerily throttled gasp spat out from those shadows and then another so close that the two sounded as one. Rocco Lucindo kept on moving sideways though sort of punched over from the top and going down head-first into a sliding dive, his big meaty paw convulsed around the holster and all his claims to life bubbling out of a shattered skull.

Regret fled and gratitude took its place as Spinella frozenly contemplated the curiosity of sudden death.

Where did a guy go in that fleeting instant, in that abrupt transition from life to death?

Where was Rocco Lucindo now?

Carlo did not have the answer to that. He only knew that *he* was still *here*, and it was a moment to celebrate, not mourn.

"How many more?" the big guy wanted to know.

"They're all out front with the cops," Spinella quickly replied. "Except Ripper Dan Aliotto, he's out back with the car."

"Is Ripper Dan a cool wheelman?"

"Yeah, he's the best there is."

"So get dressed," the big cat instructed in that icy voice.

So where was Rocco Lucindo now? It was a dumb question. Rocco was dead, that was all. The question to be considered now was where the hell was Carlo Spinella *going*.

But it was not, he knew, a time for idle questions of any nature, nor was it a time for arguing, dealing, or wheedling.

It was a time for *truth*, then for *going on living*.

And a minute or so after the untimely demise of his

old friend Rocco, the titular boss of the nation's capitol was in a lockstep with the Man from Death, moving through the house out the rear, down the steps toward the garage, unquestioningly and gratefully going on living.

Yeah. It was a time for understanding exactly where a guy stood ... and exactly how he could go on standing for as long as possible.

This Goddam Bolan wasn't shitting around.

8: MANHUNT

Ripper Dan was a "cool" wheelman, all right. He eased the big sedan through the assemblage of official vehicles, intermittently sounding his horn and exchanging wisecracks with the uniformed patrolmen until they were clear of the congested area, then sent a worried smile into the rear-view mirror and asked the men behind him, "Okay, now what?"

"Virginia," came the crisp reply from the big bastard who sat beside the boss.

"Yeh, take route 29," Spinella muttered. He quickly added, "Play it straight, Ripper. This's no time for fun'n games."

The wheelman nodded his head in understanding. There had been no need for that note of caution. Ripper Dan had recognized Mack Bolan at first shiver, let nobody wonder twice about that.

Where the guy had come from, and how he had managed to get the drop on Carlo and Rocky inside their own joint—these were not questions of anything more than idle curiosity. The only fact of immediate interest was that the guy was sitting back there with a big blaster snuggled into Carlo's armpit. It wouldn't take much to set the thing off—a twitch, a hard sigh, even—and Ripper Dan had a large respect for that big cold bastard back there. He'd as soon kill both of them as to wait and wonder why they twitched or sighed.

He kept both hands high on the steering wheel, both of them always in clear view. Carlo was directly behind him. Bolan was off to the side a little, with an unrestricted angle of vision into the wheel area.

This placement also gave Ripper Dan a good view of Bolan, via the mirror. The guy was really something else. He didn't really look too much like those posters, that artist's sketch. A little, yeah . . . but a lot of guys could look like that sketch. Only one guy could look *this* way, though. It didn't really have too much to do with the shape of the face or the way it was put together. It was something *under* that face, something inside those eyes, that a guy identified as Mack Bolan.

Yeah. The guy was something else.

Ripper Dan suppressed an apprehensive shiver. He was scared, sure. He could admit that to himself. His hands were clammy and there was a ball of mush or something right at the top of his stomach. Sure he was scared. This guy had death written all over him. How many goddam people had he killed already? Hundreds, easily. Maybe thousands. And it showed.

But there was something different about the guy.

Dan Aliotto, after fifteen years with the mob, had known a lot of professional killers. He even ate supper once with some of the old Murder Incorporated bunch. They'd been hard bastards, too. But not like Bolan. There was something different about this guy.

Ripper Dan wished that he could put a finger on that difference. He could not. And it bothered him. Why should it bother him?

Unconsciously he shrugged his shoulders and sent another quick glance into the mirror. His eyes met those cold blue ones from the back seat, the gazes locked for an instant, and something passed between them.

What? What was that message?

Ripper Dan did not know. But he thought he understood a bit more, now, about that *difference*.

Respect.

Yeah, that was it. You just instantly *respected* this goddam guy. Not the uneasy fear kind of respect which Aliotto had usually felt for the professional killers. You respected those guys, sure, but in a different way. All the time you were respecting them, you were also putting them down in your own mind. When you were around guys like that, you just automatically felt *better* than them. Weaker, maybe, but still better. Bolan did not affect a guy that way. Bolan made you feel *lesser* than him. Yeah, that was the difference. He made you remember your own sins, not his.

How about that?

Ripper Dan tried another glance in the mirror, and his gaze snapped back with a confirmation of his new truth. Shit, you could almost *like* that bastard . . . gun and all.

He cleared his throat and told the guy, "You said Virginia. It's a big state."

"Don't fuck around," Carlo fussed. "You know where he wants to go!"

Another silent message crackled across the polished surface of that rear-view mirror. Ripper Dan understood that one also. Sure, he knew where the guy wanted to go.

"Wrong place," he volunteered, ignoring his boss entirely. "Gus's got about twenty boys guarding that joint. It's like a fortress, electronic eyes and everything. You don't want to go there."

The ice-edged voice replied, "I'm not. Carlo's going."

Whatever the hell that meant.

Ripper Dan felt rebuffed in his attempt at casual friendliness. So maybe he had mis-read the guy, after all. Besides that, he could feel the seething eyes of Carlo Spinella boring into the back of his head. It was a rather discomforting feeling.

The wheelman turned his full attention to the chores of navigating the streets of early-morning Washington. Moments later they were crossing over into Virginia and speeding into the countryside.

The balance of the journey was conducted in total silence. It was nearing seven o'clock when Ripper Dan pulled onto the access road leading to Riappi's Virginia joint.

It was a ten-acre estate, walled—totally isolated

from its surroundings—further buffered by a golf course to the north and empty fields in all other directions. A narrow macadam drive ran about a hundred yards from the access road to the gate, a massive hunk of iron bars which could be opened only by electronic controls from inside the walls.

The place had always given Ripper Dan the shivers. It seemed too much like a prison, especially for a guy who had spent much of his early youth behind walls like those.

"Stop here," commanded the icy voice from the rear.

They stopped there, just inside the drive, still nearly a hundred yards from the gate.

In a barely audible voice, Spinella told his captor, "Hey, pay no mind to Ripper Dan. I can get you in there if that's what you want."

"Get out," Bolan ordered, ignoring the offer. "Both of you."

Carlo Spinella was the first to touch the turf, Aliotto following quickly and exiting on the same side of the vehicle as his boss.

Bolan was standing beside the car on the opposite side. "On your bellies," he commanded. "Arms and legs spread."

Shit! Were they going to get it right here, laying on their faces, a bullet in the head? Another front door delivery?

Spinella was gasping out a weak protest but complying with the order.

Bolan transferred the Beretta to his left hand and

hauled out a big silver autoloader with a ventilated barrel.

Ripper Dan found himself marvelling at the huge weapon, unwillingly fascinated by the probable instrument of his own death. Why the switch in guns? Some sort of ceremonial bullshit? Dead was dead, wasn't it?

He had heard reports on this big handgun of Bolan's. They called it an AutoMag—meaning, Aliotto supposed, an autoloading magnum—a .44 caliber and the most impressively powerful thing going in handguns. It was supposed to be equal in every respect to a big-game rifle—and yeah, Ripper Dan had heard the amazing stories of what Bolan could do with that cannon.

He was surprised by the coolness of his own voice as he told the self-appointed executioner, "I'll take mine standing up."

The guy told him back, "You can take it in both kneecaps if that's what you want."

Aliotto winced, glanced at his boss who was now spread-eagled on the ground, and replied, "Okay, if that's your style. But I want to see it coming."

The guy was looking past Ripper Dan, not at him, the cold gaze traveling the hundred yards or so to the gate.

Two of Riappi's hardmen had come out of the guardhouse and were standing down there inside the iron bars, interestedly watching the goings-on at the front approaches.

What the hell? Couldn't the goddam jerks see the goddam big gun in the goddam guy's paw?

Spinella was gurgling, "This's dumb, Bolan. What're you going to accomplish by this? Those boys will be out of there and chasing your ass all over Virginia."

The big guy calmly replied, "Not *those* boys, Carlo."

The stainless steel cannon came up and out, extended at shoulder level in a firing-range stance, and a pair of thunderbolts shook the air in tandem explosions and annihilated the distance between the car and the gate, and the two hardmen down there were instantly jerked erect, doubled over, and flung back clear out of sight—all of it coming so quickly that Ripper Dan did not immediately understand that it was *them* and not *him* who had been shot.

Both of Aliotto's knees buckled. He had to steady himself against the fender of the car to keep from falling over, himself.

Spinella had rolled to one side and was stabbing a hand into the air as though trying to ward off an attack . . . and suddenly he understood, also.

The thunderous reports of the big gun were still churning the air around them and Spinella was muttering "Jesus, Jesus" when the man in black spat out his final instructions.

"Go tell Riappi, Carlo. I don't want his nickel and dime operation, not this time. I want Lupo. Tell him that, Carlo."

"God okay, yes, I'll tell him!" Spinella cried.

Those eyes clashed with Ripper Dan's, and they told Ripper Dan to get the hell back inside the car.

The wheelman did so without a word. Bolan moved into the front beside him.

Aliotto spun the vehicle about in a digging U-turn, then sent it accelerating smoothly toward the main road. He told the big guy at his elbow, "You're something else."

He received no reply. The guy was swiveled toward the rear, watching the abandoned Carlo Spinella's frenzied dash for the sanctum of Gus Riappi's hard-site.

Carlo had a handkerchief in his hand. He was wildly waving both arms above his head, probably fearful of drawing defensive fire from inside.

But Ripper Dan knew—it had all come too fast. Nobody down there would be reacting before Carlo could get close enough to be easily recognized.

Ripper Dan Aliotto was not wasting any worry on Carlo Spinella. Carlo was the lucky one.

Or *was* he?

Aliotto told Bolan, "Maybe I can help you some, guy."

The icy voice replied, "Maybe you'd better, guy."

"You want Lupo, huh? That's the one you want?"

"That's the one," was the cold response.

Yeah. Maybe Ripper Dan Aliotto was the lucky one.

By eight o'clock on that Spring morning in the nation's capital, the entire community was buzzing with the news of the latest brand of excitement in this city of perpetual excitement. Election year politics and other local preoccupations took the back seat as columnists and commentators, congressmen and diplomats, bureaucrats, lobbyists and all who composed the governmental community turned undiluted attention to the dramatic visitation of the man in black, Mack Bolan.

A radio commentator on a national morning news show allowed, "There are ripe grounds here for the Executioner to plow", adding, however, " . . . it seems unlikely that Mack Bolan, if indeed he is in Washington, will live out the day in this bastion of police power. It bears pointing out that Washington is the most policed city in the free world. Besides the more than five thousand municipal policemen, an amorphous mass of federal lawmen consisting of Secret Service, Capitol Police, Parks Police, Military Police, and FBI constitute the most formidable odds yet encountered by the man from blood, Mack Bolan. And if these are not enough to contain him, there are practically unlimited reserves to draw from surrounding state and county law enforcement agencies."

Another commentator quoted "sources" inside the FBI who worried about a sudden influx of "hit men" who might be swarming into the city on the Executioner's trail. "Wherever Bolan surfaces," one source pointed out, "the head hunters and bounty killers are usually not very far behind. My chief worry is that the streets of Washington may be turned into shooting galleries."

Developments at National Airport later that morning seemed to verify that prediction. Three separate parties of "underworld triggermen" were intercepted there during the first thirty-minute surveillance of incoming passengers by FBI agents. All were briefly detained and released after being "questioned and warned" concerning the nature of their visit to the national capital.

A government spokesman later admitted, "There is very little we can do to avert a showdown here between Bolan and the underworld. We are, of course, maintaining vigilant surveillance of all known criminal elements in the area. Other than that, we can only wait for another round of fireworks and hope that we are in position to move quickly and positively against the principals."

During a television news special of events of the late morning, a spokesman for the mayor's office pointed out that police apprehension of Mack Bolan was the key to the entire problem. He added, however, that normal police procedures had so far proven ineffective and would probably continue to be so.

"This man is not your run of the mill fugitive," the spokesman explained hinting that extraordinary police procedures were being activated. "We will make full use of the provisions of the 1970 D.C. Anti-crime Bill, and all elements of the law enforcement community, federal and otherwise, will be directed from a central command. As far as the Metropolitan Police are concerned, the apprehension of Mack Bolan is the number one police priority in this city. All leaves have been cancelled and the special reserve forces have been activated."

Questioned as to actual numbers of police involved in the man-hunt, the spokesman replied, "I can only say that the full resources of the law enforcement community are being utilized. This, of course, includes federal civilian, as well as military, police."

Asked about the legality of using military police in a civil action, the spokesman pointed out that Mack Bolan was a military deserter and "fully liable" to the "full reach of military justice."

Meanwhile, the nitty-gritty of police work was underway throughout the district and in surrounding areas. The city's traffic networks were partially paralyzed by "roaming and intermittent" police roadblocks. Rail, bus and air terminals were under heavy surveillance. It was estimated that half of the taxicabs in the district were being temporarily piloted by plainclothes policemen and the reception desks at car rental agencies within a twenty-five mile radius of Washington hastily were manned by attractive young policewomen.

By mid-morning, rumors had begun to filter up through the network of police informants to the effect that Bolan's initial lightning strikes into the Washington underworld had netted considerably more than the seven dead victims thus far discovered. Stories were being passed around which indicated widescale panic and wholesale defections within the local crime organization. It was said that a local Mafia chieftain, one Carlo Spinella, had abruptly disappeared with all his cadre—and it was being whispered that the "big boss" of the district, Gus Riappi, was barricaded within a nearby Virginia estate with "a small army" to protect him.

Several precinct captains also reported that the routine activities of various underworld cells had "ground to a halt."

"All the bookie joints are shut down tight and we haven't seen a numbers runner on the streets all day," one captain declared. "This guy has put the fear of God in them, I guess. What he did to their counterparts in Boston last week is still too fresh in the mind. But it's making our job tougher. The word is out all over town that this guy is stalking, and they're all simply dropping from sight. We were hoping to use them as bait to do some stalking of our own."

Another police spokesman, who preferred to remain nameless, voiced the hope that Mack Bolan would "realize what he's up against in this town and simply drift on out. We have enough problems here already without this guy."

Mack Bolan was not, however, drifting on out.

He was engaged in a manhunt of his own, pursuing the job in his own inimitable style.

He was looking for "Lupo."

He was prepared to track the guy into hell itself.

9: THE DAY OF DAYS

That section of Massachusetts Avenue which briefly parallels the Rock Creek and Potomac Parkway in Northwest Washington is usually alluded to as "Embassy Row." It is from here that the greatest concentration of foreign powers assembled anywhere in the world conduct their diplomatic liaisons with the U.S. Government.

It must have seemed entirely fitting to "J.A. Carrico," then, that the IMAGE headquarters also occupied space in this distinguished company.

Known in some quarters simply as "Lupo," Carrico was a registered lobbyist and director of IMAGE (Institute for Minority Action Group Encounters). A thirty-two-year-old lawyer of Italian descent, Carrico had appeared on the national scene "from nowhere" a short time earlier, taking over as national head of the lobbying group. He had remained a background figure, however, with most of the direct lobbying activities being carried out under the guidance of a veteran Washington "counselor," the influential and widely respected Milton Campbell.

101

Lupo enjoyed referring to the three-story converted mansion on Embassy Row as "the embassy" and he actively promoted the idea that IMAGE was "the first class voice of America's ethnic-class citizens" in their representations for "a fair deal in this supposedly democratic country."

In reality, IMAGE was nothing more than a convenient front organization for the political designs of the crime combine and, in that capacity, served as the closest thing to a diplomatic mission which could be realized by an underground operation. The diplomacy being conducted from the old mansion on Embassy Row was, however, of a decidedly different cut than the usual brand of international pussy-footing. Even the most casual visitor sensed that a very determined war was being waged from those musty, shuttered rooms—a war of no ordinary dimensions.

The address on Massachusetts Avenue had been the national home of IMAGE since its inception some two years earlier, but only in recent months had the activities there reached the present feverish pitch of concerted excitement.

The entire top floor of the building was partitioned into small office cubicles, each equipped with a desk and a private telephone, from which most of the routine contact work was conducted. Each cubicle was manned by an energetic young man with flawless academic credentials and very persuasive manners.

Lupo referred to these as "the bull rooms."

The second floor was divided into two huge, open areas with desks arranged back-to-back along one side, long tables and bulging file cabinets spotted for maximum space utilization on the other.

Lupo laughingly called this area "the legislature."

Twelve lawyers and dozens of male "clerks" worked grimly and silently here over stacks of GPO publications, congressional records and copies of legislation currently pending action or introduction in the U.S. Senate and House of Representatives.

The ground floor of the institute housed a gracious atmosphere for reception, entertaining, and "above-board" conferences with legitimate elements of the Washington community.

Much of the basement area was given over to "the archives"—a super-security area where secret documents and records of "successful lobbying" were stored in heavy vaults. Armed guards commanded the entrances and no one entered this area without proper credentials.

The "sweat rooms" were down there, also—sound-proofed cubicles which could serve as detention cells, interrogation rooms or whatever might come up in the nature of "hard business." These rooms were seldom used except in the dead of night, and most visitors to the area arrived either unconscious or blindfolded.

The basement was also the site of "Studio City"— another heavily guarded and elaborate setup for still photography, sound recording, and video-taping— complete with darkrooms and sophisticated electronic labs. A specially-prized and highly sophisticated item of equipment in this section was a miniaturized version of a big-city telephone exchange—from which, reputedly, a large number of Washington's official telephones were being electronically monitored and conversations recorded—all automatically.

Lupo enjoyed telling visiting bosses that the operation at Studio City had "sunk more political ships than all the public scandals combined, as far back as you want to go."

Then he would wink and drolly add, "We don't uncover scandals here. We manufacture them."

In more private moments, the Mafia hatchet man might quietly expand upon his favorite theme: "The American political system is rotten clear through. Ideally it should be the best in the world. Actually it's the lousiest. It's a system of deception, dishonesty, downright thievery. What it boils down to is simply this: in a country this size, government by the people is a physical impossibility. A government official or an elected representative knows he can't please all of the people all of the time, and usually he doesn't even try to please any of the people any of the time. He gets cynical. He sees that every human being is out for just one thing—his own self interest. The electorate, yes, that's who I'm referring to. We vote for the guy who we think will look out for *our* own best interests. Right? Well, a guy gets cynical. He figures, what the hell, the labor people are looking for nothing but favorable labor legislation. Businessmen care for nothing but legislation and policies favorable to more and better profits. Vote *black* and you make friends for life with one-tenth of the electorate. Look good in social security and you've wrapped up the Geritol set. Be kind to Honkies and Wops and you've got a nice power base there.

"It's all one big game of special interest. This is a nation run by the interplay and conflict of special interests. The politician knows this, and he learns damned quick how to start looking out for his *own* special interest. So he concentrates on pleasing those who can do him the most good or at least he puts up an appearance of doing so. Actually, he's just looking out for Number One, and he's going to grab off everything he can along the way.

"I figure these people are fair game. If they're for sale, and they are, then I figure we have a right to a seat on the political exchange."

At this point Lupo may laugh then continue with, "What the hell, it's *our* franchise, isn't it? If these guys want to play dirty pool then they've got to play by *our* rules. Sure. Those guys are fair game. I'll take them any way I can."

One such take-over was being engineered in Studio City on that fateful morning of Mack Bolan's incursion into the national clout routes.

A video-taping production was underway.

A nervous man of about thirty was seated behind a prop desk, visibly sweating under the glare of studio lighting as he gazed soberly into the lens of a video camera.

An off-camera "examiner" was asking leading questions. The "witness" was giving his replies with every show of sincerity and credulity:

"And so, as a licensed private investigator in the state of New York, you were employed by the congressman's wife in such a capacity?"

"Yes sir. She was thinking of instituting a divorce action, you see, and she wanted to have the ammunition before she showed her hand."

"But a divorce action was never filed against the congressman. How do—?"

"The reason for that will become obvious, sir. My investigations of Congressman Fuller turned up some very shocking—"

"Please confine your responses to direct replies, Mr. Turner. Acting as an agent for Mrs. Paul Fuller, you did proceed into an investigation of her husband?"

"Yes sir, I did."

"Was there some particular direction to this investigation?"

"Yes sir. Mrs. Fuller suspected her husband of having a clandestine affair with another woman. She asked me to ascertain the facts in the case."

"She suspected her husband of marital infidelity?"

"Yes sir. She was hoping to find evidence of adultery."

"I see. And did you in fact uncover such evidence?"

The witness smiled grotesquely. "In a manner of speaking, yes sir."

"Please explain."

"On the evening of January 14th, this year, I tailed Congressman Paul Fuller to a motel on the outskirts of Lakeside, New York. The Starlight Inn."

"The congressman registered there? Under his own name?"

"No sir, he did not register at all. He proceeded directly to cottage number four, knocked and was admitted."

"Then you have no documented proof of this visit by Congressman Fuller to the Starlight Inn near Lakeside on the night of January 14th?"

"Yes sir, I do have. In cases like this we always give careful attention to such details. I have the documentation."

"And what is the nature of that documentation?"

The "detective" held up an enlarged snapshot which he identified as having been taken by himself, using an infra-red camera. It showed a cottage of the motel variety, with the numeral four easily distinguishable on the door, and the sharp profile of a man entering the cottage. "I took the picture and I have an affidavit from an employee of the Starlight Inn attesting to the validity of time, date and subject."

"And you have found in your experience that this manner of documentation will hold up in a court of law?"

"In a divorce court, yes sir. This method of documentation is standard procedure in my business. We have a method of marking the film for identification purposes without removing it from the camera, these very special cameras, sir."

"I see. Please continue."

"Well I gave him about ten minutes to get settled." The witness leered into the video camera. "Then I busted in, using a front window for entry. That's when I took *this* picture."

Another enlarged snapshot appeared on the studio monitor, in close-up. The detail was exquisite. Two nude persons were depicted, in a bedroom setting, standing in a passionate embrace.

"You'll have no problem identifying Congressman Fuller," the "detective" declared, smirking. "The other man is a well known fairy queen from Lakeside, a gay prostitute. You can understand why Mrs. Fuller decided to drop *that* hot potato. They have two kids."

The balance of the "interview" had to do with "irrefutable" documentation and matters of identification. When the taping was completed, Lupo went into the lab to inspect the quality of the video pickup of the enlarged "snapshots."

"Pretty good," he told the technician, after studying the results.

"As good as you'll ever get," the video man assured him. "I airbrushed the original overlays through three reproductions of the negatives. I'd challenge anyone to prove it a phony."

"No need for that," Lupo said. "If this doesn't keep the smart-ass in line then we'll just take him *out* of line entirely."

"Okay. Standard two prints?"

Lupo growled, "Yeah," and returned to the production area. He was awaited there by Raymond La-Curza, his good right arm.

LaCurza's usually expressionless face was twisted

into an unhappy scowl as he hurried over to intercept the boss.

"What kind of bitter pill are you sucking on?" Lupo asked his lieutenant.

LaCurza growled back, "It's stamped with a big B and it's not Bayer, but that's pretty close. It's this goddam Bolan, Jack."

"What's the wise-ass into this time?" Lupo asked disgustedly.

"He's into Washington, that's what."

Lupo's scowl faded. He took the other man by an elbow and steered him into a sweat room, carefully closed the door, and calmly demanded, "Okay, let's have it."

"I told you about the Vitale hit last night. I sent the crew around to cancel it. I told you—"

"Sure, sure, you told me. So what about Bolan?"

"That's what I was getting to. It wasn't Matti's crew that hit Carlo's boys, after all. It was Bolan."

"Who told you that?" Lupo asked quickly.

"Hell it's all over the news. He left his calling card. He got to Matti, too."

"How much damage?" Lupo snapped.

"All but the wheeler, Vasquez—this Bandalero Vasquez, the Puerto Rican kid. And he's been—"

"Screw him!" Lupo snarled. "What about the woman?"

"The Vitale babe?" LaCurza shook his head. "Hell, I don't know, I didn't even think. Far as I know. . . ."

"Find out! Let me know right away. I want that woman and I want her all in one piece!"

"Sure, boss, we'll run it down. About Vasquez. He's been flooding the contact setup with urgent calls. He—"

"Then contact him," Lupo commanded. "With a crew."

"You mean . . .?"

"Of course I mean! You don't want that guy running around loose, not with Bolan on the prowl. Take care of that first—right away. Then get me a scrambler hookup to New York, you know where. I'll tie Bolan's ass to a pole but good!"

LaCurza wheeled about and headed for the door.

Lupo called after him the instructions, "And don't forget the woman! Don't you mess that up again!"

The lieutenant threw a reassuring nod to his boss as he passed through the doorway.

Lupo followed him out and went directly to the "studio." He beckoned his production chief to his side and told him, "I want that Harmon Keel package before noon today. Don't screw me around with alibi's and reasons why you can't. I want it *today!*"

The producer sputtered, "Without the broad, Mr. Carrico, I don't see how we can wrap it."

"You wrap it, that's all. Dummy it, fake it any way you have to. You just deliver *today.*"

The man went away shaking his head and Lupo headed up the stairs to his office.

He was met there by Andy Lucchia, his personal secretary. Lucchia was twenty-eight, a graduate of Columbia law school and more recently a CIA operative in Cambodia. His present duties included doubling as a bodyguard for his boss.

"Heard the news about Mack Bolan?" Lucchia inquired sourly.

"I heard," Lupo replied. "Raymond is setting up a contact with New York. Put it through to me immediately."

The secretary acknowledged the command with a curt nod. "This could be very serious," he said, his mind still obviously on Mack Bolan. "Do we still go with all engines full ahead?"

"We go," Lupo replied heavily. "And we snatch off Mr. Bolan's head on the way. Soon as I get through with New York, get Milton Campbell on the horn. We're going for the grand slam this evening."

"*This* evening?"

"You heard what I said, Andy." Lupo continued on into his private sanctum and locked the door behind him.

Damn right, he was thinking. A whole army of Mack Bolans couldn't stop the master timetable now. Not even the U.S. Army could alter the course of history which was shaping up in this town on this day of days.

Bolan could be an irritant, sure, a troubling thorn in the side. But the guy would go the way all the others had gone . . . down for the count and groveling in the dust at the conqueror's feet.

This was the Day of Days . . . for the Thing of *all* the Things.

It had been carefully prepared and long awaited.

And now it was here.

This was to be the day when the American government went underground. And the day when the so-called *invisible second government* of the nation would be the only *real* government.

10: COUNTEROFFENSIVE

Bolan had changed into a pale blue spring-weight suit in anticipation of quitting, for the last time, the tiny efficiency apartment which he had engaged in Washington's northwest section.

Claudia Vitale, devastating in hot pants and a hiplength cape, stood rigidly at the window and watched the tree-lined street below.

Ripper Dan Aliotto was squeezed behind a small dining table, appreciatively eyeing the girl at the window.

Bolan made a final adjustment to his gunleather and closed the coat over it. "Time to move out," he announced. "Any second thoughts, Ripper?"

The Mafia soldier reluctantly shifted his gaze from the girl to the tall man with the piercing eyes. He coughed nervously and replied, "I've come this far. I might as well go all the way."

"You'd better understand this, soldier," Bolan told him. "I'll let you walk out of here right now, free and clean. You get in your wheels and take off, no strings, and that's that. If you stay, though, and I get the feeling later that you're doubling on me—well then you're in trouble."

"Sure, I know," Aliotto muttered. "I said I'll go all the way."

Bolan's eyes flashed in what could have been taken as a smile. He said, "Okay." The gaze traveled to the girl. "Claudia?"

"I'm in," she replied in a muffled voice.

"Same conditions," he told her.

She had not budged from her position at the window. "I know. I'm in."

"Okay." Bolan moved toward the door. "Let's go, Ripper."

Addressing Claudia again as Aliotto scraped to his feet, Bolan told her, "Start your backtrack as soon as we're out. Limit your telephone time to ten minutes at any given location, then move on to another. Keep your spiel to the point and don't give any one contact more than a minute or two of your time. Tell them just enough to assure a continued interest."

She murmured, "I know what to do."

He said, gruffly, "Sure you do."

"I won't let you down," she said, turning to him with a sober little smile.

Aliotto moved between them on the way to the door, and Bolan was glad for the intervention. He turned away without meeting her gaze and busied himself with the implantation of a false mustache, then he added sunglasses and followed Ripper Dan into the hallway.

"Damn it, be careful," the girl called after him.

114

He replied, "That goes double for you," and pulled the door shut.

Aliotto grinned and told him, "I think you got yourself a gal."

Bolan said, "Not by a damn sight. But I'll settle for a reliable ally."

"Oh hell, you got that, too," the Ripper assured him.

"Just play it straight, soldier. I'm getting to like you."

The dark Italian face broke into a huge grin. "Me too," he said. "But I gotta say, I never expected to be gunning with Mack Bolan."

"Start calling me Frankie. Start getting used to it right now."

"Sure, Frankie."

"And you're not gunning. You're just driving and spotting."

"Oh hell, I couldn't do it any other way. I never hit anybody in my life and I'm getting too old to start now."

Bolan let that pass, though he guessed that the truth was being stretched a bit. They went past the elevator and headed for the stairway.

Aliotto said, "Uh, that babe back there. . . ."

"Yeah?"

"She, uh, she belonged to Smilin' Jack Vitale."

"I know that," Bolan said tightly.

"Did you notice the freeze she had on for me? They'd been married only about a year when he got gunned. You know, the trouble up in Boston. So she's

115

got no love for the organization. I thought you might like to know that. She thinks we're all cutthroats." The Mafia wheelman shrugged and went down the stairs ahead of Bolan. "Maybe we are," he added, peering over his shoulder to catch Bolan's eye. "I can see why she'd feel that way. She didn't even have the consolation of crying over her husband's grave. He got buried, I hear, in a cement coffin about a mile at sea."

The guy was trying very hard to establish a personal relationship. Bolan gave a little and asked him, "What was Vitale's thing?"

"I dunno, he was just made, fresh out of college. One of those new-wave types, you know, like Lupo. None of the old bunch liked those types, I guess. I mean, it's our money that puts these fresh new-wavers through their fancy colleges. You know, the money from the streets. Then they turn around and bad-mouth us. Say we're out of date, stuff like that. I guess that's why Vitale got it. Too damn fresh. Nobody liked him much, I hear."

"You didn't know him personally?"

"Oh naw, they were with the Boston family."

"So was Lupo," Bolan commented.

"Was he? I didn't know."

The two men reached the ground level and headed for the rear exit to the parking area. Ripper Dan fell in beside Bolan, all smiles as he struggled to match the long strides of his companion.

"How the hell tall are you, anyway," he huffed.

Bolan ignored the query. "Something is off center," he said, the voice barely audible.

116

"Off center where?"

Bolan pushed the door open and nudged Aliotto outside. "Not here," he replied. "Somewhere else, never mind. Go get the car. Circle the block twice. Pick me up in front, second go-around."

The wheelman nodded his head in understanding and went on alone.

Bolan remained inside and watched through the partially open doorway as Aliotto entered the car and drove away. He held the surveillance for thirty seconds then went back through the building and out the front exit.

It was a routine precaution, a rear-guard defensive procedure which he had learned in another kind of combat zone and one which had served him well in this new brand of warfare.

The VC's had been a wily and dangerous enemy.

But no more so than this new enemy. America still produced some of the toughest fighting men in the world, regardless of which side of the law they happened to land on.

Bolan had a huge respect for the combat instincts of this American underworld enemy. Carelessness had no part in his combat operations—and perhaps this accounted for his successes so far.

It was a hell of a grinding way of life, though. There was no let-up, not ever, no relief from the minute-by-minute necessity for remaining alert and combat-ready—and there were no sanctuaries, no place or time—not even a frame of mind in which he could let down completely and simply relax and let the world turn unnoticed.

But ... it was still his bag. He'd picked it out and then shouldered it, knowing that he would be stuck with it for as long as he remained living—and that he would remain living only so long as he continued carrying the load.

Relaxation meant sudden death.

There were times, now and then, when that sole sanctuary—death—took on an appealing appearance. Even at those times, though, that stubborn ferocity of spirit which had so characterized the man would not allow him the simple luxury of dying.

There was a hell of an important job to be done.

Death would be a cop-out. It would mean not only the end of Mack Bolan but, in some permanent and perhaps irreversible way, it would mean the loss of something very important to the human situation— something very important to an evolving universe.

Bolan did not overemphasize or glamorize his own role as a sentient fragment of that universe.

He simply knew that, somehow, what he was doing was of tremendous importance ... and he quite simply accepted the responsibilities of the role he had undertaken.

Now he was in Washington, involved in some sort of climactic moment of this do-or-die responsibility.

Yes, he could feel the battle-lines drawing in upon him, tightening around him—and yes, very definitely something was off center and clamoring for his attention, something which now was hovering at the edge of his consciousness and demanding to be noticed.

But there were many very tangible dangers, also, demanding his full attention. He could not withdraw to the battlefront of pure mind to examine the subliminal warning cries. In this sort of existence, a practical warrior faced the exigencies of each present moment and he rode each heartbeat as though it could be his last.

This Mack Bolan was doing. He watched Ripper Dan cruise by in the first pass of the pickup point and satisfied himself that there were no tail-cars in the following traffic.

A couple of minutes later he was sliding in beside the newest recruit in his "War Against Syndicated Cancer" and they were moving swiftly toward a new battlefront.

In the apartment which they had just departed, another recruit was beginning a painful backtrack along a trail of fraud, blackmail and vicious intimidation. Claudia Vitale was "doing her wash"—contacting her list of "victims," explaining all and soliciting support for Bolan's war.

Phase Two of the counteroffensive was off and running.

11: SEARCH MISSION

The search for an illusive shadow had to begin somewhere, and it began for Bolan at an address in a townhouse apartment complex, site of one of the recent renovations underway in the inner city.

The wheelman parked at the curb in front of a duplex unit. "This is it, Seventeen-B," he muttered. "It's the downstairs part. Has a living room, two bedrooms, kitchen, dinette. That's all."

"How many ways in?" Bolan wanted to know.

"Just two. Door in back opens on a small yard, fenced."

"How many heads in there?"

"Two. Sammy Spear and a guy they call Flash Gordon. I don't know exactly what they do, but they're somewhere in the chain to Lupo. Part of the look for these new-wavers—they're equal opportunity employers. It's not just an Italian mob, anymore."

"These guys gunners?" Bolan asked.

"Betcher ass. Mean ones, too. We had a meet here once. Carlo had to work out a contact setup for reports to Lupo."

"Reports on what?"

"Hits. We did a lot of sub-contracting for Lupo. I got the idea that these guys Spear and Gordon were the coordinators. Lupo never shows hisself personally. I never once saw the guy. More red tape than Capitol Hill. Sometimes it backfires, too. Like that deal last night, the Vitale hit. Somebody got their signals crossed. Lupo didn't want that hit. By the time the word came down there was no way to stop it."

"Okay," Bolan said. "Let's go talk to the coordinators."

The time was shortly past noon. Ripper Dan Aliotto went directly to the door and pushed the bell button.

Bolan, conspicuously flashy in the skyblue business suit and dark glasses, remained on the walkway in open view of the windows and made a show of casually looking over the neighborhood.

The door at 17-B cracked open on the second summons. A chain-lock was in place, and Bolan drew a fleeting impression of a voluptuous blonde woman on the other side of that door.

A pleasant female voice sang out, "What do you want?"

Aliotto announced, "Tell Sammy it's Ripper Dan. Urgent business."

"I'll see if he's here," the blonde replied.

While they waited, Bolan lit a cigarette and idly drifted up the walk. A deep voice from the doorway warned, "That's close enough, guy."

Bolan halted and crossed his arms across his chest.

Aliotto said, "That you, Sammy?"

"Yeah. Where's your boss?"

"Over in Virginia."

"Yeah, so I hear. Who's your friend?"

"That's Frankie Lambretta. We gotta come in Sammy."

The door clicked shut momentarily then rebounded fully open. The voice from the inside was farther removed now as it called out, "Okay, come on in. One at a time."

Aliotto smirked at Bolan and stepped into the apartment. The cool man in blue followed close behind, blowing a cloud of cigarette smoke ahead of him.

Sammy Spear stood in the center of the room with a snubnose revolver trained on the doorway. He was a man of about thirty, medium height and build, wearing rumpled dress slacks and a shirt open at the neck, gunleather suspended from the shoulder.

Another man was also present. He was similarly dressed and armed but his weapon was sheathed. Obviously a bit younger than Spear, Flash Gordon wore muddy-blond hair in a fuzzy "Afro" style. He held a drink in one hand and a cigarette in the other; he was leaning casually against the back wall.

The buxom blonde had retreated to a couch. She wore nothing but bra and panties—with very little fabric to either. Strikingly pretty in a brassy way, Bolan read her as sex on the hoof—any time, any place, any way.

He also had a flashing rear view of another girl,

equally undraped, as she disappeared through a bedroom doorway.

Bolan casually turned his back on the entire scene to close the front door and restore the chain lock. When he turned around again, Spear was sheathing the revolver and walking toward a small portable bar in the corner.

The gunman paused in mid-stride to snap an irritated command to the fall-out blonde: "Go get something on!"

The girl flounced out of the room and Spear went on to the bar and poured a hefty slug of bourbon into a glass.

"This is getting on my nerves," he announced to no one in particular. "If you boys want a drink, help yourselves. Bartender is off duty."

Aliotto read the eye signal from Bolan and replied, "Thanks, we ain't got time."

The man at the back of the room drawled, "That's all we have got." He was obviously a southerner, with a twangy high-pitched voice. "Y'all sure that sergeant sonnabitch isn't on your tail?"

"Shut up, Flash," the other man muttered.

Gordon grinned at Aliotto and said, "Sammy don't like to be reminded. A Ghost Who Walks is in town, and my buddy Sammy is haunted." He laughed, raised his glass in a silent toast, and took a deep pull at the drink.

Spear ignored the gibe from his partner. "What d'you boys want?" he asked the visitors.

"I got orders to contact Lupo," Ripper Dan truthfully replied.

The "coordinator" shrugged and told him, "You know how."

"Not anymore. It's all gone ka-flooey. The whole town has buttoned up."

The southerner was staring fixedly at Bolan.

The Ghost Who Walks casually removed his dark glasses, dropped them into a pocket, and stared back.

The other gunner was telling Aliotto, "That's tough shit. I hear your whole bunch has holed up in the country."

"That's the problem," Aliotto admitted.

"Well that's your tough shit. We're on Condition Red security and it's going to stay that way."

Aliotto complained, "Well, geez, how the hell're we gonna ...?"

The southerner chuckled, his gaze still interestedly on Bolan. "This dude here looks familiar. Who is it, Frankie what?"

The man in the blue suit spoke for the first time since entering that apartment. The icy voice advised, "Frankie nothing. The name is Bolan."

Flash Gordon started a nervous laugh, then snapped it off and very slowly moved the cigarette to his lips and left it there.

The man at the bar dropped his glass to the floor and carefully moved both hands onto his belly. He growled, "Don't screw around. That's not funny."

In a flattened voice, the southerner declared, "He's not screwing around. It's him, all right."

Moving nothing but the muscles required for speech, Spear said, "Ripper, you son of a bitch."

Bolan was simply standing there at stage-center, legs spread, arms hanging casually at his side, coat open, the Beretta visible in her snapaway rig.

"Get clear, Ripper," he quietly commanded.

Aliotto casually dropped into a chair near the door, a strained smile masking his emotions.

Sammy Spear's voice was showing its tension as he said, "Easy, easy. Let's understand just what we got here."

"You've got trouble," the cold tones of the Executioner informed him.

"We all got trouble," Spear replied. "But nobody's blasting yet. So ... what do you want?"

"I want Lupo."

The southerner let out a shaky chuckle. "You can't have him," he said, but not very convincingly.

"So I'll have you boys instead."

"Which one?" Flash Gordon blustered. "One is all you're going to get, if that much."

"Try me then."

"Hold it, dammit," the other gunner demanded. "This's all a lot of bullshit, anyway. We don't know nothing to tell you."

Bolan said, "Too bad. That was your only out."

A strained silence took over the room, magnifying the situation. Small sounds which ordinarily would go unnoticed became almost clamorous—the ticking of a watch, a fly buzzing against a window pane, the

125

movement of air through constricted breathing pas
sages.

Bolan gave the moment full head, allowing adren
alin-charged muscles to tense and fatigue, encourag
ing nervous systems to overtax and deteriorate—and
then he told them, "Time's up. Start talking or slap
leather."

Sammy Spear made the first break, and he made
the mistake of trying it cowboy style, spread-legged
and flat footed.

Bolan had him measured, aligned, and timed—and
the Beretta Belle was leather-free and spitting her
soft song of doom before the challenger's hand had
closed around his weapon.

The Parabellum hi-shocker crunched in squarely
between Sammy's bugging eyes and punched him
over backwards onto the bar, his dying gurgle lost in
the crash of bottles and the splintering of the cheap
wood.

The second silent round was already tracking Flash
Gordon as he catapulted sideways toward the bedroom door. It smashed into his gun arm and spun him
around just in time to catch another sizzler in the
throat—and gun and man continued the death
plunge, crashing into the door and on through to the
bedroom floor.

Ripper Dan Aliotto was poised motionless half in
and half out of his chair, his face an emotionless
blank.

Bolan muttered, "Damn! Strike out."

126

In a hushed voice, Aliotto told him, "Depends on your point of view, I guess."

The blonde woman, still clad only in the abbreviated panties and bra, lurched through the open doorway from the bedroom. She had evidently been in the receiving line for Flash Gordon's geysering blood, and she was wearing it in rivulets about her upper body. The pretty face was twisted into a grotesque mask of horror and shock.

Bolan holstered the Beretta and warned her, "It's no better out here."

She was already well unglued before her eyes settled on the ugly sight on the opposite side of the room. "God, you shot his eye out!" she wailed.

True enough, one of Sammy's eyes had popped from its mutilated socket and bounded halfway across the room. It lay there, bloodied, iris up, streamers of shattered nerve tissue coiled about it.

Ripper Dan dropped back into his chair with a shuddering, *"Jesus Christ!"*

Bolan took the blonde's arm and led her back to the bedroom. The other girl, a cool-looking redhead, was standing woodenly over the crumpled remains of Flash Gordon. She had pulled on a pair of bluejean hip-huggers but was bare from the hips up.

Bolan steered the blonde around the mess there and shoved her toward the bath. "Clean yourself up," he suggested.

The redhead turned to regard him with a cool gaze. "Why'd you have to do this?" she asked him, in

127

a voice which could have been inquiring about the time of day.

Bolan wondered fleetingly if she was narked-up, then quickly decided that she was not.

Maybe it was not a total strike-out, after all.

He shrugged and quietly responded to her inane query. "War is hell. I'm looking for Lupo."

She said, "I know. I heard it all. You're out of luck. These guys were nothing. They wouldn't know Lupo from Margaret Mitchell."

"Would you?"

The woman shook her head. "I'm nothing, too. I work for him, sure, like this poor jerk here did. But so what? We're layered, see, and I mean *layered*. This is the lowest layer. I don't know how many more there are between here and Lupo. Loud and clear?"

Bolan told her, "Loud and lying. I've never shot a woman. But I might start."

She stared at him for a long moment, and what she saw there apparently brought her mind to a sane decision. She sighed and told him, "Oh hell, it's not worth it."

She stepped away from the gore beneath her and made bloody barefoot tracks to the bed where she dropped to her knees and dug something from beneath the mattress.

When she stood up she was holding a small leather folder which she thrust at Bolan.

"If what you want isn't in there, you'll just have to start shooting," she said. "It's not much but it's all we ever had."

Bolan opened the folder with one hand and riffled the lined pages inside, then he moved immediately into the living room and told Ripper Dan, "Bingo. Let's go."

Aliotto preceded him to the front door without a word or a backwards glance.

The redhead came in behind them and called to Bolan, "You're a real hard son of a bitch, aren't you!"

He turned to look at her as he was going through the doorway.

"I try to be," he said, and gently closed the door on Lupo's lower layer.

12: THE MAN

It was precisely three o'clock in the afternoon when Ripper Dan dropped his passenger on the east side of the Lincoln Memorial.

The tall man in the blue suit, mustachioed and wearing dark glasses, immediately struck off through the trees lining the Reflecting Pool.

He was awaited there, several yards into the trees, by a powerfully built man on crutches.

The meeting with Harold Brognola had been pre-arranged that morning.

The Justice Department official's first words to the most wanted man in the country were, "Who do you think you're fooling with that get-up?"

Bolan smiled soberly and replied, "Myself, maybe."

"You're sure standing this town on its head," Brognola sourly observed. "I wish you'd move a bit softer. You're diverting a lot of attention from the critical points."

Bolan knew that, and the worry expressed by Brognola was not exactly alien to himself. He said, "Yeah. It's starting to pay, though." He produced a folded sheet of paper from the breast pocket of his coat and gave it to the other man. "Don't bother studying that right now, I only have a minute or two. It's an organization chart showing the pyramid of power in the local operation. Trouble is, most of the blocks are blank. All I have filled in are about the lower three levels. And I'd hate to tell you what I had to do to get that far."

"You're working on the others, though."

Bolan sighed. "I am."

"I've been getting calls all afternoon, from a lot of greatly embarrassed people. Are you behind that, too?"

Bolan told him, "Maybe. Which people?"

"Hell, I won't go into names. But the list includes congressmen, civil servants, members of executive and congressional staffs—one, even, from the White House staff. All with a similar story. They'd been duped, compromised, and blackmailed by a young woman on Harmon Keel's staff. They would talk to me and only to me. I got the same suggestion from each of them—as though they'd been coached. A secret meeting, a *group* meeting, to discuss ways and means of exposing the operation."

"Did you set up the meeting?"

"Sure I did. Eight o'clock tonight. You knew about it, eh?"

Bolan said, "Yeah. Keep it quiet, eh. There's something rotten in your own house."

"Are you," Brognola snapped, "telling me? It's like

walking across wall-to-wall marbles. But don't worry. I'm playing all cards very close to the chest. Incidentally, for what it's worth, I'm going to be walking your side of the street from here on, even if I have to resign and walk it as a private citizen."

Bolan said, "Don't do that." He gave his unofficial friend a tight smile and added, "Speaking of walking, how's the leg wound?"

Brognola had picked up an unintended bullet in the thigh while attempting to nail Bolan to a casino wall in Las Vegas.

He returned the smile and told his favorite fugitive, "It's okay. I'll be ditching these crutches in a few days." It was obviously an embarrassing point. He averted his gaze toward the Pool and growled, "Hey, I was temporarily insane at Vegas. It's a condition called *dementia bureaucratis.*"

Bolan chuckled. He said, "Forget it. I have. What can you tell me about a lower echelon hood called Smiling Jack Vitale?"

The Justice man's eyes flashed in recognition. "Vitale is a name I've been hearing all afternoon," he snapped. "That's the woman in the case."

Bolan told him, "Smiling Jack's widow. I need to know exactly how long she's been a member of Keel's staff, how she got there, the whole bit. Also I'd like to know if her husband ever worked for Keel, when, and in what capacity."

"You said widow. The guy's dead, then."

Bolan nodded. "He was with the old Boston mob.

132

The story goes that he got caught in the middle of the factional dispute up there. But something is off center. I need a full profile on the guy."

"Okay, I'll run it down."

"Keep it quiet."

"Sure. How will I get it to you?"

"I'll contact you."

Brognola rubbed his nose and said, "Okay. This is getting pretty hairy, though. I don't even trust my own telephones anymore."

"You shouldn't," Bolan told him. "I keep getting rumbles about a fantastic intelligence network at work here."

"Electronic eavesdropping?"

Bolan growled, "Yeah. A very sophisticated refinement of the game. And I keep bumping into ex-CIA people. This guy Lupo has pulled together one hell of an effective operation."

"No clue yet to Lupo's actual identity?"

Bolan shook his head. "Not yet, but I'm getting closer. Ever hear of a country, Costa Brava?"

Brognola stroked his chin for a moment before replying. "Seems like. One of the small Latin American republics."

"It's more like a municipality," Bolan said. "It began as two small islands in the Caribbean—privately owned property. Through some mysterious international hijinks, it has emerged as a constituted nation." He grinned, adding, "Population one hundred and twenty. But they have tentative recognition in the

133

UN and a diplomatic mission here in Washington. Can you buy that?"

The Justice Department man snorted. "At this stage, I'll buy anything. What's the connection with Lupo?"

"I don't know that yet. But wouldn't it bo a sweet setup for the mob? Picture it. A nation of their own, less than an hour by plane from Miami. Political sanctuary, diplomatic immunity, financial freedom for illegal bucks, the whole trick."

Brognola swore softly. "And a retirement village for elder *Mafiosi*, eh. Yeah, I'm buying it more and more. The traffic south has been growing heavier all the time. But what's the local connection?"

"Immunity, maybe," Bolan replied. "Their mission is in the middle of Embassy Row. Small but neat—and who could ask for a better cover?"

"You think you'll find Lupo there?"

Bolan said, "No, not there. It's just another block in the pyramid. But a rather strategically placed one, I think. I'm going to hit the place tonight."

Brognola put on a wry smile and commented, "You don't recognize diplomatic immunity."

"There's no immunity in my jungle," the Execution-er softly declared.

"Yeah, well ... it's been nice, Pointer. Uh, use that in your contacts with me. Scramble it good when you're talking. You know the routine."

They shook hands, and the man from blood walked quickly away.

The meeting had consumed only a minute or two.
But it had been refreshing as hell.
That was a *man* back there, he was thinking.
Where the hell were all the others?

13: PACERS

The pace of the Executioner's war on Washington shifted from deadlier to deadliest immediately following that mid-afternoon meeting with Harold Brognola. A series of strikes, obviously planned and timed to perfection, sent shock waves through official Washington and brought on "a crisis" in the unified police establishment.

The first target of that new round was a fashionable residence in the city's northwest section, not far from Embassy Row. It was the rented home of "Jaffie" Little, a budding Washington socialite who had risen to national prominence as "the Pearl Mesta of the younger set."

In the words of the police lieutenant who headed that investigation, Bolan "rousted Miss Little, forced her to open a wall safe, terrified several female house guests, and shot dead in their tracks two security officers employed by Miss Little."

Bolan himself would later report to Harold Brognola, "You can fill in another block and name it Jaffie Little. She's been supplying drugs and sex for the VIP beautiful children, catering specifically to the diplomatic community. I smell an underground UN operation, built on the same brand of intimidation they're using on our federal people. Fill in the block and then cross it out. Jaffie Little is now out of business. And, oh yeah, get word to the people in New York. Jaffie's counterpart there is a gal called Trudy Hamilton."

The trail from Jaffie Little led to a physical culture "spa" in Georgetown. The official police report from that sector used the terms "bloody rampage" and "wholesale carnage" in describing that strike.

"This was no hit on the Mafia," declared a federal officer. "Bolan just ran wild in there, slaughtering innocent civilians. I don't see how any of his apologizers can justify this one. He gunned down four reputable citizens in a sauna room and another six in the recreation area. Those last six he tossed into the swimming pool after he shot them. These ten victims were all highly reputable attorneys engaged in various lobbying and counseling activities in and around the capitol. None of them were armed. Some folk hero. He shot those people down in cold blood. Then he robbed the place."

Bolan's report to Brognola had a different ring. "The Georgetown Gym and Health Club is the home away from home for Lupo's inner circle. It has been the nerve center for coordinating the interlocking operations. I discovered this much: that club is the revolving door into Lupo's home operations. Every member has direct access to the top of the pyramid.

But you'll have to cross off ten of them. I found out that they had reached the last few hours of their countdown. Things are much worse than I would have believed this time yesterday. Lupo actually has the country in the palm of his hand. All he has to do now is close the fist. I'm doing my damnedest to keep it open, but its getting very gory. I need some help. Get some people off their asses, will you? Spread the word, this one is for all the marbles. I'm sending you some captured documents by special messenger. And get a good look at this messenger, Hal. The guy is going to need all your protection if he lives through this. His name is Aliotto. Take care of him for me."

Twenty minutes after the hit in Georgetown, a lone man in a pale blue suit walked into an office in the Federal Triangle and calmly gunned down two minor officials of the Health, Education and Welfare department. He left a marksman's medal behind and vanished in the resultant confusion.

Ten minutes later the same man put in an appearance at the Supreme Court building, executed an "important employee of the Court," rifled an office, and made good an escape in a waiting car despite the fact that more than a dozen federal marshals took up pursuit.

This pattern continued until five o'clock, ranging across the length and breadth of the city, and involving a total of eight such lightning strikes against specific targets.

A spokesman for the unified police activities hinted during a special news briefing at 5:15 P.M. that a shakeup of the police command was in progress, announcing that Treasury Agent Jim Williams was now heading up "the special command group responsible for stopping Mack Bolan's rampage."

A commentator on a nationally televised news program at six o'clock that evening mentioned "uneasiness" in the White House itself, but he went on to point out that "the quality of police cooperation" which had emerged in that city was "historically unique"—and the newsman predicted that Bolan would be "stopped" before another dawn.

"As a standard format in the development of folk hero myths," the commentator went on, "the saga of Mack Bolan is at long last beginning to drag upon the rocky shores of bitter truth. The tale had to turn this way. There could be no acceptable alternative. Once launched upon the path of bloody retribution, any self-propelled and self-elected quote champion of the people unquote must ultimately discover the final truth about himself. He is not God. Being human, he errs. And however any of us may feel regarding the American justice system, trial by jury, duly constituted authority . . . whatever . . . it is certain that tonight a nation shall weep over another of its folk myths turned sour.

"Mack Bolan today stands revealed as simply another tragic zealot who tried and failed to play God. He is the victim of his own vendetta. He is a common murderer, no matter how exalted his personal ideals, and he shall be brought to justice. That is not a prediction . . . *that* is a foregone conclusion. And, yes, we the people will undoubtedly go on weeping over our lost gods."

Bolan put the case to his personal diary in this fashion: "I'm not in this for votes or decorations. I killed a hell of a lot of people today, and I won't pretend to feel good about that. But I can't feel bad, either. Every one of those guys were rotten to the core, forget their impressive titles and offices. They were rats. And yes, damn it, I shot them out of the barrel. The battle has hardly begun, though. I still have to find Lupo."

The search for Lupo was also the subject of much anxious conversation in another quarter of Washington. In a private cubicle deep within the bowels of IMAGE headquarters, the object of Bolan's feverish search was taking reports from his general staff.

Raymond LaCurza advised his worried boss, "I'm telling you, the guy has gone plumb wild. Everywhere he stops he leaves bloody meat and the message, *I want Lupo!* He's after your ass, and I mean he's *hot* for it. He's already knocked off half of our operation. I'm telling you, we can't afford to sit around and take it any longer."

"What would you suggest we do, Raymond?" Lupo quietly inquired.

"I dunno," the right arm murmured.

"You dunno," Lupo mimicked. "You can't even find Claudia! She's been calling every son of a bitch in town and you can't even run her down!"

"She hasn't stood still long enough," LaCurza complained. "That broad is no dumbbell, Jack. I'm telling you. . . ."

"You're telling me horse-shit," Lupo growled. He stabbed a finger toward his intelligence chief, a young-old man in a wrinkled shirt who wore the dreamy look of an absent-minded scientist. "The professor here tells me she dinged fourteen numbers on our watch list. She spilled her fucking guts all over the place. And every one of those numbers turned right around and called this guy over in Justice, this Brognola fink. They're starting up a dialogue, Raymond. That's what they're doing. They're putting their heads together. And all because of our little Claudia. I told you I *wanted* that bitch, Raymond!"

The Chief of Staff shuffled his feet uncomfortably and made a half-audible reply.

"What'd you say?"

"I said let 'em talk. We've got them by the balls, anyway."

Another man commented, "Those balls are getting very slippery, though. Brognola is a bastard. There's not a handle anywhere on that guy."

"I guess we got some trouble," LaCurza admitted.

"Exactly!" Lupo grumbled. The usually genial face was set in a deep scowl. "So let's hear some suggestions."

"Pull back," the dreamy-eyed intelligence boss offered. "We've lost the fine control already. Even if you got to Bolan in the next five minutes the timetable is crippled and wobbly. Maybe beyond immediate repair. I say pull back. Regroup. Wait. Let the fur settle. Nothing has actually changed. Most of our casualties had become expendable, anyway, at this point of the proceedings. We still *have* the clout. The thing to be decided now, the way I see it, is simply *when* to exercise it."

"This timetable is no arbitrary thing, professor," Lupo argued. "We have to observe the realities of the political schedule. The primaries are breathing down our necks already."

"Well ... my suggestion still stands."

"All right, that's one idea," Lupo said. "How about another?"

LaCurza muttered, "I agree with the professor. We've come this far on finesse. I don't see what we'll gain by trying to bulldoze the thing through now, what with all the waves this Bolan has made."

"I never saw a sonuvabitch operate like that," another member of the board commented. "Like a buzz saw. That guy gave us more grief in one day than we've ever known all combined."

"He's a bastard, all right," LaCurza agreed. He stared blankly at his boss. "One thing the professor overlooked, talking about our expendables. A lot of those were our *muscle*. We don't have a hell of a lot left. I mean, not the kind you'd want to use in a delicate operation like this one."

"Yeah, there's that too," Lupo agreed. He sighed. "That Bolan is a ... a...."

"He is a phenomenon," the intelligence man said quietly.

Lupo turned his full attention to the "egghead." He

stared at him thoughtfully for a long moment, then asked him, "How do you go about neutralizing one of those phenomenons, professor?"

The man smiled and replied, "Pure energy cannot be destroyed. It can be diverted. It can be transformed, or absorbed into inert matter. But it cannot be destroyed."

"Well you better translate that for me."

"How many men in the organization have died trying to destroy Mack Bolan?"

"Too damned many," LaCurza put in.

"Exactly," the "professor" agreed. "So why keep on pitting one energy source against another? Obviously Bolan's energies are superior to the best we can field against him."

"So?" Lupo growled.

"Absorb him."

"Wait a minute, now," Lupo replied in a slow drawl.

The intelligence chief was smiling and nodding his head. "Let the idea find its level."

"You don't mean we should *buy* him," LaCurza said. "That's been tried before."

"No, I wasn't thinking of that. Simply absorb him into the operation. The same way we've absorbed so many others. Let's get some *face value* out of this energy source."

A borning smile was pushing the scowl from Lupo's face. He lit a cigarette and sent the smoke in a gusty exhalation toward the ceiling. Presently he said, "Well I'll be damned."

"I don't know what the hell he's talking about," LaCurza groused.

Lupo was positively beaming now. "*Face* value, that's what he's talking about," he declared, the humor returning to his voice and punching it up to its usual bounce. "We'll put so much heat on that bastard he'll run screaming clear out of the damn country. If he can *get* that far."

"What the hell're you talking about?" LaCurza demanded.

"I believe he's thinking about Faces Tarazini," the professor said quietly.

"What's *he* got to do with anything?" asked another man at the table.

It was LaCurza's turn to start grinning. He chuckled and said, "Well God damn. How come nobody never thought of that before?"

"I guess nobody *had* to before," Lupo said, still all smiles. "What time is that meeting, Professor? That fink session with Brognola?"

"Eight o'clock," the intelligence man promptly replied.

Lupo stabbed a finger at him. "Okay. Call the headshed in New York. I don't care where Faces is, I want him here by eight o'clock. I don't care if he's in Istanbul or at the south pole, I want him here before eight. They can steal a military jet or whatever it takes, but I want the guy *here*."

The professor rose quickly to his feet. "You'll have him," he assured the emerging boss of Washington.

"What does all this have to do with Bolan? asked the mystified member of the council.

"Tarazini used to be an actor," the professor told him, as though the simple disclosure would answer all questions, and then he quietly left the room.

Lupo laughed and waved his arms over his head. "Jesus, I don't know where I get these beautiful ideas. Can you *imagine* that bastard's face when the shit hits the fan? He thinks he's been having it rough? He thinks the cops have been hard at his ass just for knocking off a few criminal types here and there? Jesus!"

"Yeah, that's rich, that's really rich," LaCurza agreed, shaking all over with the immensity of the idea.

"I still don't get it," the third man said.

"Don't worry, *Bolan* will!" Lupo howled. "Hey, Raymond. Wouldn't you love to see the bastard's face when he realizes he's been absorbed?"

"I don't get it," the complainer repeated, feeling left out.

Lupo was riding high, and in no mood for explanations. "Hey, Raymond, what if Bolan decides to knock off the fucking President, eh?"

"Oh, my ass, that's too *much!*" LaCurza shrieked.

"We just might have him do that," Lupo said, suddenly very sober. "Yeah. Yeah. What the hell? Maybe we'll just do that."

An entirely new pace—and perhaps a whole new game—was being introduced into the war for Washington.

145

14: THE QUESTION TO THE ANSWER

Bolan had posed a metaphysical riddle to himself during the Boston adventure, and only now was the solution to that mystery beginning to slide into focus.

Bolan had learned that the eternal question of metaphysics is, everywhere, *why*. Not how, not when, not what—but, forever, *why*. Even a small child unconsciously knew that. Why, Daddy? Why is the sky blue? Why is it dark? Why is it raining?

And the Executioner had found himself wondering....

New York City was the financial center of the country, perhaps even of the entire world. Yet Bolan had found there not a highly organized conspiracy to dominate the financial scene, but the master plan for *Cosa di tutti Cosi*, the Big Thing, political control.

Why? Why in New York, the financial nerve center of the nation?

Las Vegas was unquestionably the gaming capital of the American continent. But there he had found not a looming conspiracy to dominate all gambling interests everywhere—instead he discovered vast sums of black money skimmed from casino profits and diverted in an unending torrent to buy political favors and influence in virtually every section of the country—and outside it.

Why? Why political ambitions in Las Vegas, the goldenest goose of gaming in all the world?

In the Caribbean he had stumbled onto a tropical paradise, an area ripened and ready for full exploitation by the tourist industry. But the Mafia bucks there were not moving into resort hotels and island casinos, not the bulk of it. They were going into—what else?—political power bases.

Why? Why politics in paradise?

What was so goddam *big* about politics?

Sure, it was comforting to have influence in the power centers. But how much comfort could a guy stand? How much could he afford? Were these guys paying out all that sweaty money just for *comfort*?

No, hell no; Bolan had already come to that decision long before Boston.

He had seen in Chicago what could be accomplished when the businessman, the politician, and the gangster were indistinguishable one from the other.

But it had taken Boston to bring the full dimensions of this insidious master plan into true perspective. . . . Bolan had wondered . . . if New York were the financial center, Vegas the gaming center, Washington the political center . . . then what the hell was Boston?

Why did that city figure so prominently in the big

scheme? *Why* the life or death struggle there for dominance and supremacy?

And now, in Washington, the puzzling and eternal game of insoluble riddles was leveling out.

The answer to *why* was focusing-in as *why not*.

The answer was paradoxical, sure, like all metaphysical truths.

Why not take over?

They had the money.

They had the people.

They had the power.

So . . . *why not take over?* Why fool around with *political influence*, with more *comfort?*

They could have the whole crumbling cookie!

Why dick around with the game of politics, that uncertainest and most unpredictable of all human pastimes?

Why even finance a political machine which is dependent upon the goodwill of the people when you can *build your own perpetual monster* and suck up all the votes everywhere?

Sure. Let the suckers vote.

Why not?

All candidates will be servants of the monster.

Yeah. Oh yeah. And here was a God who would give the people stones when they ask for bread. You bet your ass.

So . . . *why* had become *why not*.

And the solution to the riddle then became so painfully damned simple.

There was no reason WHY NOT!

As for the question of Boston and why did she figure ... another of the paradoxes emerged.

She figured because she did not figure.

She figured because it had all *started* there.

The mastermind of the master plan *was a Bostonian.*

His code name was Lupo ... *the actual name could be anything.*

Harmon Keel came from Boston.

So did Claudia Vitale.

And a man sometimes called Lupo, also, came from Boston.

The old city figured because she did not figure. It could be no other way. A Boston background was considered prestigious, in some circles. The nation had originated there, in many senses. The fine old patriot bloodlines descended from there, as well as some highly repsected political families.

Sure. Double damn sure. She figured because she did not figure.

The riddle, thank God, at last was solved.

And Bolan thought he knew who Lupo was.

But Lupo, he had also come to realize, would not be his final goal in Washington. That ultimate target would be someone straight, someone fine, someone prestigious and patriotic, it would be someone from respected political stock.

The Executioner would find Lupo, yes.

And then he would have to find *the man behind Lupo.*

He would have to find the man who was being groomed as the next President of the United States.

The problem had to work that way because it was the only solution to both sides of the paradoxical equation ... a mob President was the only answer to both *why* and *why not*.

And the Executioner shivered over that truth.

He would have to hit that guy.

There simply was no question to the answer.

15: ABSORPTION

Bolan met Claudia Vitale, by pre-arrangement, at seven o'clock on the steps of the Library of Congress. He took her hand and they strolled like lovers to the Court of Neptune, the marvelously sculpted bronze fountain, where he sat her down atop the railing and they gazed into each other's eyes and murmured soft words in the manner of lovers everywhere ... but these were not words of love.

"I hear you got it set up," he told her.

"Yes. I believe most of them will be there."

"You too, Claudia."

"Sure. I'll be there."

"You've got a selling job. Convince them. Fight back or get eaten, that's the message. There is no accommodation with this enemy, no halfway house anywhere in their plans. It's all or nothing. Let's make it nothing. Tell that to your pigeons."

"I'll tell them. I know what to do."

"I know you do. Just do it, eh. This may be the last chance."

She wriggled under a light tremor. "It's kind of scary, the way you say it."

"If you think it's scary now, wait until the cannibals take over. They'll eat us all alive."

"I know that. Still, I guess I never really faced the reality of it. You know . . . sometimes it's easier to just drift along and hope."

He said, "Claudia. . . ."

"Yes?"

"This is going to sound square and corny, but . . . how did a nice girl like you . . . ?"

She laughed softly. "It's corny only because it happens so often, I guess, to so many people. I don't know how I got in this deep, not really. Just drifted in, I guess. First it was Jack, and—"

"Your husband."

She soberly nodded her head. "Yes. He was a rat, I guess. I didn't see it then. Oh . . . I had stars in my eyes. Political Science major, you know. Jack was . . . older and glamorous. It was Harmon's—Congressman Keel's bi-annual scramble for re-election and I was one of those nutty kids very long on ideals and very short on common sense."

"You were working for Keel when you met Vitale?"

"No. *He* was. Drumming the campuses in our congressional district, looking for volunteer campaign workers." She smiled grimly. "I got hooked . . . on both Keel *and* Jack. Anyway, we went from one warm thing to another. It was my senior year. We won for Harmon, I graduated in the Spring, and I became Mrs. Smilin' Jack Vitale in June."

"When did you find out?" he asked her.

"Find out what?"

"That you'd married into the Mafia."

She screwed her face into a thoughtful, frown and told him, "Well I'm Italian too, you know. I believe I knew it all along. I just wouldn't face it. But then . . . after we returned from the honeymoon and I became a full-time member of the staff—"

"What staff?"

"Harmon Keel's staff. He keeps an office in the home district, you know. Jack ran that office for him. And I went to work for Jack. I started seeing the under-the-table deals, the payoffs and all, and of course I knew, then. And there were the constant parties, the secret meetings with known hoods, the seemingly unlimited supply of money and all the nicer things of life. On an administrator's salary! I had to see it, then."

"Did Harmon Keel know, Claudia?"

She shook her head. "I'm sure that he never knew. He doesn't know to this day. That's one of the. . . ."

"What were you going to say?"

She made a wry face. "I guess I didn't want to bring it up. I . . . I've grown to love that pitiful old man. Keel, I mean. He's like a grandfather to me. We have this thing, you see, this unspoken thing. Especially since Jack died. I believe it would kill Harmon if he should learn the truth about me."

And Lupo used that as a lever on you?"

"Do we have to talk about this right now?"

He nodded his head firmly. "We do."

She murmured, "Well, sure, he used it. Continually.

153

After Jack ... was removed ... things suddenly began blossoming for me. I mean, career-wise. I moved very quickly from the very lowest desk of administration at the home district level to where I am now ... Washington chief of staff. I didn't know at first, though, that someone else was pulling my strings."

"And that all started after your husband died?"

"Yes. I've often wondered, too, if that was *why* he had to die. I mean, Jack had become compromised himself. He had become 'known'—I mean, identified by his mob connections. Too many local people knew. It was beginning to restrict his movements."

"So you figure the mob removed him and began promoting you."

"I've wondered about it."

"When did you take your first dive?"

Her eyes blanched. "You mean beneath the bedcovers? Let's not talk about that, please. Not you, Mack, please. I'll tell anybody else you say, but...."

He growled, "Okay. But I'm struggling for the pieces to the puzzle, Claudia."

"That part of me is no puzzle," she said in a very low voice. Then, obviously steeling herself, she went on. "I just sort of slid into it. My first dive, as you call it, was entirely innocent on my part. I mean, I didn't know I was being used. For God's sake, I'd been a widow for two years. I'm not ... *old*, Mack." She took a shuddering breath and continued. "Well they had my place wired ... for sounds and sights. And they got plenty of both. I was sort of in love with the guy,

154

and I still believe that he was serious about me." She shrugged her shoulders in a delicate little gesture. "*They* killed that, *oh boy* did they kill it. A short while later, Lupo arrived on the scene and then my strings *really* got a jerking. Pretty soon I simply didn't care anymore. I didn't care about anything. I did what they told me, without a quiver. Until. . . ."

Bolan said, "Okay, I have the picture."

"It sure is a dirty one," she murmured.

"But getting cleaner all the time. Keep it going. You're doing great."

They parted moments later, Claudia to keep a rendezvous with her conscience—Bolan to keep a date with death.

Yes. He had the picture now.

The time was eight o'clock and the place was Harold Brognola's modest townhouse in Georgetown. The full list of invited guests had arrived and had clustered into small groups of quietly self-conscious compatibles.

Brognola came in with Claudia Vitale, who was making a brave effort to keep her chin high and her eyes sparkling. Without preamble the meeting was called to order and the serious business of salvaging a number of once-promising political careers got underway.

Claudia had her say, holding the floor for most of twenty minutes, and it was a brutal recitation of encroaching national doom.

Then Brognola added his official comments, recommendations, and assurances that "this whole thing can be smoothed out and made right."

The sticky details of individualized "scandals" were not discussed, but Brognola passed around a "logbook" and asked for signatures "to cement the common bond and to signify a willingness and a desire to stand up and fight back."

Eleven of those present signed the logbook. The other three expressed an unwillingness to commit themselves "at this time," though promising to keep the matter under consideration.

At about 8:40, the meeting broke up.

Claudia Vitale remained in her chair, sipping a glass of sherry, while Brognola saw his guests to the door.

It was a black night, moonless and starless, and no one was aware of that other presence in the darkness outside until the fireworks began. The solemn group was clustered about the small porch and short stairway, saying goodnight, when a tall figure in total black stepped from the shadows of the yard into the glow of the porch light.

He tossed a metallic object onto the porch; it clattered against the side of the house and fell into the crowd.

Brognola cried out, "Mack, for God's sake, what are you doing?"

And then an automatic weapon which the man in black was holding began its chilling chatter, and the group on the porch went into dissolution.

Two of the guests staggered down the stairs and made a run for the darkness. They were promptly chopped down.

Harold Brognola, his face streaming blood from a flying chip of brick, dodged back into the house and returned the fire with his revolver.

The attack ended as abruptly as it had begun, and when the shooting was over, fourteen men lay sprawled across the porch, the stairs, and the lawn. The man in black had vanished.

Two junior United States Senators and a Congressman died there at Harold Brognola's front door.

A top congressional aide and an official of HEW died minutes later, enroute to the hospital.

A prominent political committeeman, an FBI administrator, three law clerks assigned to the U.S. Supreme Court, and three other officials in high levels of the executive branch sustained non-mortal wounds.

And as the final ambulance departed the scene, Harold Brognola, his face streaked with dried blood from his own minor wound, turned to a shaken Claudia Vitale and dropped a marksman's medal into her hand. "I can't believe it," he croaked. "I simply cannot believe this."

At that grimly dismal moment, the man from Justice would have given both his legs to know that the man who left the marksman's medal was not Mack Bolan, but an ex-actor known as Faces Tarazini.

Mack Bolan was being "absorbed."

And while the police were still churning up the neighborhood in the vicinity of Brognola's home, the whole city and ultimately the entire nation was electrified by the news that "at approximately nine o'clock this evening, a man believed to be Mack Bolan, firing from an as-yet-undisclosed location, sent a fusillade of high-powered rifle bullets through several windows of the White House. There were no injuries, repeat, *no* injuries to the President, his family, or to any members of the White House Staff."

Yes, the man from blood was being thoroughly absorbed.

16: MOVEMENTS

While the city buzzed with the latest shocking developments and the outraged official clamor approached fever pitch, the real Mack Bolan piloted his warmobile out Massachusetts Avenue and onto Waterside Drive in a penetration of Rock Creek Park. He left the vehicle in good concealment just west of Embassy Row and doubled back on foot, a black-clad moving shadow of a foreboding night.

The Executioner was combat-ready. He wore the tough, skintight blacks with matching ripple-tread shoes. The Beretta Belle nestled in her shoulder holster beneath his left arm. The impressive silver hogleg, the .44 AutoMag, lay snug in flaptop military leather, suspended from a web belt at the waist. Four small fragmentation grenades also dangled from that belt, and in his leg sheaths were stiletto, incendiary flares and extra clips for Beretta and AutoMag.

He was ready for war.

The Costa Brava "diplomatic mission" was housed in a smallish mansion snuggling with the more impressive embassies lining Massachusetts Avenue, their backsides reaching out toward the park. He came in through the rear, scaled a rock wall and penetrated several hundred feet of turf to the garages without incident.

There he experienced an incident.

Some dude was lying on a garage roof and breathing rapidly through congested nasal passages.

Somebody, Bolan decided, should send a Care package of *Sinex* to the Costa Bravan delegation.

He doubled back to the wall, scaled it, and began again, this time directing his advance along the top of the wall itself, moving on hands and knees and with the utmost care along the side of the property to that point where garage roof met rock wall.

He stepped aboard and moved cat-fashion to the peak, easing down on the guy with the Beretta extended onto the opposite downslope.

"Freeze," he suggested in a voice just above a whisper.

The guy stopped breathing momentarily, then turned his head slowly toward the sound of doom. Twenty seconds ticked across Bolan's mental clock, then the guy whispered, "Well—fuck me. Is that Mack Bolan?"

"I am. Who you?"

The guy raised to all fours and began a slow crawl up the incline. Bolan allowed it, but cautioned him, "Carefully."

Yes, there was something familiar about that face—but it had been only hastily glimpsed under tense conditions, and Bolan was sliding it across his mental

160

mugfile when the guy told him, "You don't know me. But we met already, God did we. I was wheeling that hit on the Vitale cunt last night."

Bolan said, "Do tell."

"Yeah. Name's Vasquez. They call me Bandalero."

"What are you doing holding down this roof, Bandalero?"

"Say, you wouldn't believe it."

"Try me," Bolan suggested.

"Them lousy bastards sent a crew after me."

"What lousy bastards?" Bolan delayed the response with a hand over the guy's mouth. "Talk quiet if you intend to live on."

"Sure. I was talking about Lupo and company. I just had a feeling, I knew by the way they gave me those dicky instructions for the meet. They were setting me up."

It wasn't making much sense, but Bolan asked him, "Why?"

"Hell, I don't carry a card. I'm no blood brother to those guys. I just take orders and four bills a week. Guess they figured they didn't need me anymore, not with Frank Matti dead and gone."

"So you still haven't told me what you're doing here."

"I won't put up with that crap, that's why. I figured to find Lupo and have it out with him, face to face. Besides, they owe me a week's pay."

"Keep talking, soldier."

"Well I got around a lot with Matti. A wheelman

sees a lot that ordinary soldiers don't see. I brought the guy here a lot of times."

"You brought him *here*?"

"Yeah. I figure there's a connection somewhere."

"What makes you figure that?"

"I mean, a *real* connection. A tunnel or something, to somewhere. Twice I remember Matti bitching about a dark hole and why the hell didn't they furnish bicycles or something. Also he didn't like the way they treated him. He was growling around about having to use the servant's entrance, like he wasn't good enough to be seen going in the regular way."

"Going in where?"

"Hell I don't know. But it wasn't *this* joint."

"So did you find the tunnel?" Bolan asked.

"Me?" The Bandalero seemed confused. "You mean, did I go inside there looking for one? Hell no, not me. I just figured to lay up here and wait for something to show."

"You're the guy with the shotgun," Bolan told him.

"Yeah, I. . . ." A streak of raw fear traveled the full length of Vasquez's face in a slow advance from the eyes to the mouth. He said, "Whatta you got, a photographic brain or something?"

Bolan told him, "Or something. Where's your boomer?"

"Down there."

"Down where?"

"Edge of the roof. Layin' in the gutter."

"Okay. Leave it there and split. Come up this way, down my side, onto the wall, and haul ass for the

162

park. Don't dawdle and don't look back. Above all, don't come back."

"Say, are you hitting this joint?"

"What do you think?"

"I think I'd like to hit it with you. I'm pretty good with that scatter-gun."

Bolan pondered the offer, but only briefly. He had pushed his luck too far already this day, dealing in both Claudia and Ripper Dan. He told the little guy, "Thanks, but I work alone."

Vasquez seemed almost relieved by the turndown. He said, "Yeah, sure. Why argue with success, huh? Well listen. I been staked-out here since just after dark. I haven't seen a goddam soul move for two hours."

"That's unusual?"

"Sure is. Anytime I was here before there was always a lot of people churning around. So take a tip from a brother. Watch your step in there. When they get this quiet, it usually means nothing good for no-body."

Bolan said, "Okay, thanks. Now move it."

The Bandalero flashed a white smile, whispered, "You're okay," then moved it.

Bolan held his position to give the little guy plenty of time to get clear, and take advantage of the delay to reorganize his own thinking.

A tunnel, eh?

He dragged out onto the surface of his mind the sketch he had made of the neighborhood earlier that day, and he scrutinized it with his inner eye until every detail was indelibly etched there.

There were three major embassies in this immediate area plus a number of institutions and private residences. The damn tunnel, if there was a tunnel, could be connecting with any of them or all of them. What would be a *logical . . . ?*

He swiveled his head northwesterly and his mind followed his eyes to the only building in the entire area which was blazing with lights from the third-story roof to the ground.

IMAGE, the civil rights outfit for ethnic minorities.

The Mafia was an ethnic minority.

And they'd been having a bit of trouble lately with their public image.

The Man from Death smiled into his inner silence and knew for damn sure that he was on a hot one tonight.

He checked his weapons, called his inner systems to full readiness, then continued his movement against Costa Brava.

Harold Brognola was a greatly troubled man, but he knew his job and he knew what had to be done now.

Whether Mack Bolan was or was not responsible for the attack on his property and for shooting up the home of the President, *somebody* was running around with a wild gun and an itch to use it—and that somebody, Bolan or otherwise, had to be stopped.

He tucked Claudia Vitale safely away in an upstairs

bedroom with a federal marshal at the door, then he went to his telephone, consulted a small red directory, and put in a call to Jim Williams, the treasury man who had hours earlier been named to take over the Bolan hunt.

Williams was an old and trusted friend, a tough gut-cop with a no-nonsense approach to his job, and Brognola knew that the turds would be in the fan now, for sure.

He waited patiently for several ring-downs across a variety of Washington offices, then the man in the hot seat was on the horn and telling him, "Glad you called, Hal, but if it's not Presidential Urgent then please hang up. I'm over my ears into hysterical officials and—"

Brognola cut him off with an unhappy snort and the angry comment, "You know damn well why I called!"

A punchy sigh, then, "Okay. If you're waiting for me to say I told you so, save time for both of us, I'm not saying it. You okay?"

"Yeah, just a nick. Jim, you need me."

"Is that an offer?"

"It is."

"Okay, get over here. I was about ready to draft you, anyway. You think you know Bolan pretty well? How he thinks, how he moves?"

Brognola sighed. "I think so, or I *thought* so."

"Okay, I'm saving you a corner of the hot seat. Move it on over here."

Brognola hung up and limped to the hall closet for

his crutches. He reached for them, glared at them, then left them where they stood and slammed the door. He steeled himself, straightened to full height, and walked briskly along the hall without limping.

Damn right, he was thinking as he moved painfully through the doorway and to the outside. The turds were in the fan now, for sure.

Brognola's car had hardly cleared the drive when the federal marshal who had been stationed in the rear yard was sapped from behind and dragged unconscious into a clump of bushes by two men with gleaming teeth and swarthy skin.

The two quickly joined a third man who waited in the shadows beside the house, and one of them asked him in a husky whisper, "What if she's not still in there?"

"Has to be," the third man replied. "The fink left by himself, didn't he?"

The trio were moving quietly toward the rear entrance.

"There's a couple of guys still in there with her. Take them out any way you have to, but for God's sake, no more shooting. The goddam neighborhood is crawling with blue."

"What if she puts up a fight?"

"Belt her, but not too hard. Raymond says she comes in one piece, you better make sure of that."

"She'll come," the other man assured his crew leader.

Lupo, it would appear, had not yet completely abandoned his timetable for the Washington takeover.

166

17: ENCOUNTERS

The house was almost totally darkened, with but two faint lights showing—one up front and another just inside the back entrance.

Bolan could make out the figure of a man slumped into a chair near that rear light. He was gazing mournfully into the tiny rectangular picture tube of a portable Sony television receiver and taking dainty, rationed sips from a coke bottle.

The Executioner came up softly behind the man and lifted him completely out of the chair, a forearm locked into the throat and the other hand clamping off nose and mouth.

The sentry died neatly and quietly while Bolan's own image stared at him from the lighted surface of the Sony and a background voice related the story of a sealed city and an angry search for the man whose likeness was being depicted there.

The front door guard looked up as Bolan advanced along the hallway. He rose half out of his chair, gawking at the apparition in black approaching him and called out a choking challenge. The silent Beretta phutted dully and the guy sat back down with a third eye not-so-neatly drilled at forehead-center.

Bolan left him sitting there and made a quiet recon of the ground-level area. He found a small office containing a battered desk and a metal file cabinet with a combination-style lock on the top drawer, so he delayed himself for a moment to open the tin can with the blade of his stiletto.

The lock-drawer held a single manila folder which in turn held several typewritten sheets of paper. Bolan scanned them quickly, then folded them and consigned them to his pocket-file.

The upper floor of the old house was totally bare—containing not a stick of furniture.

A *front* operation, he decided—and this finding served to whet his appetite for the basement level.

Down there he found carton upon stacked carton of nothing but packed earth, a small cement mixer with a gasoline engine and a trash bin overflowing with empty cement bags.

A trail of dirt and white powder led him to the doorway he was hoping to find. Beyond that was utter blackness.

The dark hole, yeah.

It was a pretty ambitious undertaking, at that.

The shaft was high enough so that Bolan did not have to bend his head to enter. His pocket flash revealed very professional shoring of the ceiling, and light fixtures at regular spaced intervals. They were still pulling wires, though, and this explained the lack of lighting. It was wide enough in there for three men to walk abreast—but Bolan had to wonder what the hell they intended to transport through that underground highway.

Yeah, a guy could ride a bicycle along that trail.

He could also penetrate what would probably otherwise be a very nasty defensive set-up.

Maybe.

At this moment, penetration was the name of Bolan's game. To hell with the maybes.

He snapped off the flashlight and went on cold, with only the back of a hand brushing the dirt wall to guide him. He counted his paces as he progressed, did his best to divine the angular changes in direction—and when he reached the door at the far end he knew that he had traveled far enough to have arrived at the Institute for Minority Action Group Encounters.

If these guys liked *encounters*, then. . . .

The door was locked. His pocket flash revealed a small button emplaced at eye level in the steel framework surrounding the door. He pointedly ignored that convenience and quietly went to work on the locking mechanism with the handy stiletto.

A moment later the catch snapped back and the door swung freely on silent hinges.

A brightly lighted cubicle-sized room greeted him. He stood there in the open doorway until the pupils of his eyes adjusted to the sudden bombardment of light, then he moved on through to the next door.

He quietly tried the knob, found it free, and went

through fast. This was a large room, elongated, with a lot of equipment at the far end.

A youngish man in sports shirt and slacks with a machine-pistol slung muzzle-down from a shoulder harness was leaning with his back against the wall, his head swiveled into the unexpected encounter and the startled eyes mere inches removed from Bolan's.

While the message was still trying to bang its way through suddenly flooded synapses, an iron forearm with two hundred pounds of push behind it pinned the sentry's throat to the wall and a fast-moving knee paralyzed the solar plexus, stilling all struggles. Those eyes bulged and rolled upwards, and the guy died there quietly pinned to that wall.

Another door, marked "Film Archives," stood to the other side of the dead man. Bolan opened it and pushed the guy inside, then laid him across a library-style table and pulled the door closed.

It was another cubicle. Except for the table and a few chairs it contained nothing but a small machine with a view-screen across the top.

Set into the back wall, though, was a vault-like door with a complicated locking mechanism featuring an interlocked spin wheel and dogging levers.

Bolan found the keys on the dead man's belt, and he carefully inspected the mechanism for evidence of an alarm system. Finding none, he followed his instincts and went on in.

It was a micro-film storage area.

Drawer after drawer of hermetically-sealed and carefully protected celluloid dynamite—a drawer for

170

each letter in the alphabet—all neatly cross-indexed for fast retrieval. Each drawer must have held thousands of miniaturized documents.

Bolan studied the index for a moment then undertook a search mission for certain files. When he found them he put them deep in his inside pants pocket.

Then he moved the dead sentry into the vault, locked the door, and added the vault key to his other treasures.

As he was striding back across the cubicle to the outer exit, that door swung slowly open and a guy leaned in, one hand on the door and the other grasping the jamb. His eyes recognized the problem much faster than the rest of him could react, for he was trying to get himself together. But there wasn't time enough left in his life to get anything together. He died there, with both arms outspread and the off-balance body tumbling on into the room.

Someone just outside exclaimed, "Holy . . . !"

Bolan stepped across the fallen man and through the doorway just in time to see another guy wheel around and take off like a track star, sprinting at emergency steam toward the far end of the larger chamber.

A nine-millimeter challenger overtook the runner at about the third stride, plowing into his neck just above the shoulders and ending the race in a face-down slide into eternity.

Both guns were in the Executioner's hands now, the big silver cannon up and ready in the right, the

171

chillingly silent Beretta in the other as he stood poised there, sniffing the atmosphere of the place like a deadly jungle cat on the hunt.

There were no sounds of alarm, no unusual movements, nothing whatever to indicate that his presence there was known among the living.

Something was going on at the far end, down in the equipment area, evidenced by moving shadows on the wall, an occasional rising murmur of voices, laughter and the general sounds of people relaxing and enjoying themselves.

At the other end of the chamber was nothingness, a blank wall about ten yards from Bolan's position and the bottom limit of an open elevator shaft.

He went to the fallen sprinter, sheathed the Auto-Mag, grabbed a foot and dragged the guy into the cubicle with the others.

As he was coming out of there for the second time, Bolan heard the whirring of the elevator mechanism. He proceeded unhesitatingly to that next possible scene of encounter and stood in the shadow provided by the shaft's framework to watch the open cage descend.

It was a slow-mover, the type used primarily to transport things instead of people—but this time it was moving people.

Two people.

The first objects to come into view were two sets of human legs—a male set, if one could still bet on pants and hard shoes—and an alluringly female set which Bolan recognized at first glimpse.

It was Claudia Vitale and a guy.

He saw her in profile as the cage settled to bottom, and there was defeat there in that slumped stance, resignation, the end of hopes and dreams.

Not so for the guy. He looked smugly happy, contented, almost triumphant.

The guy stepped out of the cage and executed one of those exaggerated flourishes which men sometimes put on for the ladies, a sort of comic Walter Raleigh act of deference—and as he straightened up his back was less than an armlength away from where the black cat waited.

He was putting her down and really rubbing it in as he announced, "*Your* level, Highness. Won't you please honor us with the pleasure of your—"

Those were all the words he had.

A surgical-steel stiletto entered his neck between the second and third cervical vertebrae, instantly severing the spinal cord and other vital matter, and the guy quietly sighed and died and oozed to the floor in front of the cage.

Claudia did not immediately comprehend. Her dull gaze rose from the instant corpse on the floor to the tall figure in black who emerged from the shadows. She cried, "Oh!"—and fell into his arms.

Bolan rubbed her back, and calmed her, then stood her aside while he tidied up the area for those who might follow. When that was done, he pulled her into the shadows and asked her, "What are you doing here?"

She said, "Oh Mack, somebody crashed our party

and shot all those people, and they're trying to blame it on you. And then they attacked the White House and they said you did that too."

He was remembering the disturbing words coming from the Sony at the other end of the tunnel, and he put it all together in a flash.

"But how does that get you here?" he wanted to know.

"Mr. Brognola went out to join the hunt." She dug into her bra with trembling fingers and produced an angular scrap of paper. "He left this number for you to call, if you should try to check back. Mack, they set you up. They're trying to make you look like some sort of maniac, attacking the President and—"

He said, "Never mind that. How'd you get here?"

"These men killed Mr. Brognola's marshals and brought me here."

"What men?"

"There were three." She pointed to the lump in the shadows. "That one. The other two came down ahead of us."

Okay. Bolan knew which men. The other two were piled into the cubicle next door.

He asked her, "What's upstairs?"

"An armed camp," she replied promptly. "It looks like D-Day up there." Her fire was returning and she was pulling it all back together. "Didn't you come in that way?"

He shook his head. "Private entrance. Okay, give me the upstairs layout, best you can."

She said, "You're after Lupo. Right?"

"Right."

"He's not upstairs. He's down here. They were bring-ing me to him."

The Executioner's head swiveled to the scene of activity at the far end of the chamber. His lips thinned and he told Claudia Vitale, "Okay, let's go give you to him."

18: IMAGES

They were lounging on one of the "sets" of the studio.

A television camera on a dolly was shoved into a corner, out of use.

A microphone boom had been left in place, hovering above their heads.

Lupo sat in a chair at a small table in the center, sharing the table surface with an electric coffee pot, a cup, and an overflowing ashtray.

Raymond LaCurza shared a stiff little couch with a much older man.

Another man, clad in night-fighter combat garb similar to Bolan's, occupied a wooden stool directly opposite Lupo. A European style machine-pistol lay on the floor beside him.

The four were watching a televised news program, laughing and commenting about information being divulged there concerning the government's now intensive war on Mack Bolan.

Bolan himself, with Claudia, was watching from an adjoining and darkened control booth, separated from the others only by darkness and a soundproofed wall of glass.

The Executioner asked Smilin' Jack Vitale's widow, "Do you know the guy in the brown suit?"

Her eyes were nearly in shock and the usually lush lips were flattened and white against her teeth as she replied, "I've seen him around. Carrico, I think, is the name."

"So what's bugging you?" he wanted to know.

"The man on the couch. The old one. That's Harmon Keel."

Bolan did not know what to say to that. Following a moment of silence, he told her, "Well it's a weird world, Claudia."

She murmured, "Yes, isn't it."

He told her, "A guy on television today said something about gods dying tonight. We have to take that sort of thing in stride."

Her lips were beginning to quiver. She said, "Yes, I suppose we do."

He knew what was running through the tortured channels of her mind. Years of deception, duplicity, cruelty, depravity, betrayal.

She had given up body and soul for the sake of that old cannibal.

Bolan would have given anything to be able to spare her the rest of it. But ... she had to learn to take these things in stride.

He told her, "Look very closely at Carrico. Study the mannerisms. Watch the way he forms his words, the way he always seems to be smiling—forget the face, look at the *man*."

She exclaimed, faintly, "Oh my God."

Gently he told her, "Plastic surgery alters only the face, not the man behind it."

The guy certainly had to be a bastard. The things he had put that girl through. . . .

Bolan saw the entire story in her eyes as she stared through a growing awareness at the husband she had thought dead for three grimy years, the agonized knowledge of marital treachery and carnal abuse.

Smilin' Jack had raped this woman's very soul, prostituted her on the high altar of personal ambition, and cast her into the hell of all feminine hells . . . and, yes, the story was written there in blood across Claudia's shuddering features.

She whispered, "So Jack is Lupo."

He said, "Yeah. Do you want him?"

Claudia shook her head, slowly, numbly.

Bolan told her, "Okay, I'm taking him."

"Let me . . . confront him first."

He said, "That would be dangerous. A lot of lead—"

"I don't care. I want him to look at me, and I want to know it's *him* looking—and I want him to know I know."

Bolan made the decision quickly. It was her right. He told her, "Okay. But remember, it's all images. The name of the *man* is written deeply inside."

She looked at Bolan then, deeply and earnestly, and she gave him one of those sober little smiles which he had grown to appreciate.

She touched his shoulder and said, "Yes. It is, isn't it."

And then she went on to confront the image of a bastard.

Smilin' Jack Lupo was laughing and telling Faces Tarazini, "You're great, you are *really* the greatest, the first guy to ever make a monkey out of—"

The declaration of brotherly love and affection got lost somewhere in the speech processes as Lupo's mind took off on another direction.

Claudia was there in the circle of light, appearing from nowhere and unescorted, and she was just standing there looking at him with a dumb expression on her face.

He slid his chair back and returned the unblinking gaze. "Well, well," he said sarcastically, "it's little Miss Finkmaster, the golden slut of Washington, come to pay us a call at last."

Harmon Keel came up off the couch, his face surprised and confused. He said, "Jack, you didn't tell me...."

"Relax, Congressman, it's the Day of Days, haven't you got that through your head yet?"

The man on the stool had swiveled about to join the party. He was leering at the girl, invading her with his eyes. "This's the one, huh?" he said expectantly.

Claudia's eyes shifted to the man in black and she told him, "I'm his wife. I'm Mrs. Lupo."

Lupo blinked his eyes rapidly, exchanged a quick glance with Keel, and reached for a cigarette.

The Congressman said, "I told you. I knew she'd peg you sooner or later."

"Mrs. Lupo, the golden slut of Washington," Claudia declared tightly. "Whatever happened to that privileged tradition of the Italian housewife, Jack? The super-care, the super-love, the sanctified bonds of tender affection and protection? *You lousy bastard you!*"

Lupo came up out of his chair fast and pointed an angrily shaking finger at her. "You bitch!" he yelled. "You rotten hotpants bitch, *you* started that shit, *I* didn't! You and your goddam bedroom Adonis, Tony Hawkins! I should've *killed* you instead of...." He decided not to say that, after all, and his eyes fled to his cigarette.

Claudia quietly told him, "You're right, Jack. You should have killed me. Now you won't be killing anybody, not ever again." The pained eyes swept across to the old man. "Nor will you, Harmon."

Lupo sat down, threw back his head, and laughed heartily. Raymond LaCurza joined in.

Keel slumped back to the couch, muttering, "I don't see any sense to any of this. Not now, for God's sake."

And then a chilling sound penetrated into the light zone from the darkness, a voice edged with ice and pitched in death. "Enjoy the laugh, Lupo. It's the last one."

The laughter ended in a strangled gasp and Lupo's hands came down flat on the tabletop, as though he were trying to imprison something there as he peered into the blackness beyond the lights.

LaCurza whirled around, digging at gunleather.

A muted, chugging report sighed across the lighted zone and something terrible happened to LaCurza's face, pieces of it splattering across the couch and onto Congressman Keel's lap.

The man on the stool was tilted sideways, trying to snatch the machine-pistol off the floor.

Another man in black stepped quickly forward and chopped at Tarazini's neck with a big silver pistol. The imposter went all the way to the floor and lay there unmoving.

Smilin' Lupo Vitale was cringing into his chair and yelling, "*I'm not armed, wait, hold it*!"

But the world had waited long enough.

An IOU had come due.

The collector had arrived.

Bolan's Beretta chugged once more, and the ivory of Jack the Wolf's smile disintegrated and went inward to seek the man, as the Day of Days came to an abrupt close for its mastermind.

Claudia had not moved, nor had she watched the second death of her husband. Her eyes were on Harmon Keel.

She told Bolan, in a voice cold and hard, "Leave this one for me. I have the best solution for traitors like this."

Bolan understood, and he agreed.

He told the old man, "You heard the lady. *Get!*"

The congressman *got*, moving amazingly fast for a

man so old and rotten inside, making terrified strides toward the elevator at the other end of the chamber.

Bolan told Claudia, "I'm going to leave his boy for you, also."

"Which boy?"

"I don't know, but you will. A presidential contender, probably. You'll know him."

She nodded. "Someone innocuous. Someone who will offer the people ease, instead of challenge. Yes. I'll take care of that one, too."

Bolan was hoisting Faces Tarazini to his shoulder. He told Claudia, "I think I'm going to need this dude. Pretty good make-up job, huh. Look at those heels. Three inches high."

She said, "Mr. Brognola will be delighted to see him." She picked up the machine-pistol. "This, too. Now, how do we get out of this tomb?"

"Just follow the bouncing ball." He grinned, adding, "That's me."

He left a trail of incendiaries behind him, and the fires were already roaring when he pulled Claudia into the black hole and secured the door.

Tarazini was coming around. Bolan set him on his feet and shoved him along the tunnel in the lead, then he snapped on his pocket flash and told the girl, "Just follow the man in black."

"I guess I'd follow you anywhere," she replied softly.

Wrong, Bolan told himself. *Wrong image.*

"Don't follow anyone, Claudia," he advised her. "Live large, and follow your own image."

She smiled and asked, "Like you?"

He peered ahead, onto the terrible wipe-out trail which had become a dark tunnel beneath the earth, and he chuckled and told her, "Yeah. Like me."

EPILOGUE

Claudia made the call to the number which Brognola had left with her, and she and Bolan stood at a window in the Costa Brava house and watched the leaping flames devour the last of IMAGE.

When Brognola arrived on the neutral ground of that "foreign mission," he was "acting as a private citizen" when he took delivery of the imposter who shot up the White House and murdered "six good men" in Brognola's own front yard. He told Mack Bolan, "I'm almost ashamed to tell you how upset I was about all that."

"You feeling better now?" the Executioner asked the man from Justice.

"These aren't tears of *sadness,* man," the tough cop replied.

Bolan added to his friend's sense of wellbeing when he turned over the papers and microfilm from his leg-file, and he cinched the thing with the keys to the micro-film vault.

"When she stops burning, I'd dig down through the rubble to the basement level," Bolan suggested. "That vault was built to ride through anything. I believe you'll find enough goodies there to turn this whole town around."

"Plus a certain senior congressman," Claudia put in. "I'll be wanting to file a formal affidavit with your office, Mr. Brognola."

There simply was not time available to say all the things which needed to be said—and there was no way to express them, anyway.

Brognola haraumphed and looked the other way while the man in black and the woman embraced, then he told his friendly fugitive, "You'll find a limousine out back with diplomatic flags flying. I believe you'll recognize your chauffeur, too. He's got some clothes for you. Don't argue with him. He knows where to take you. There is one way, and only one way, to break the seal we have around this city. We even have Riappi and his gang sealed up inside their farm, so there's nothing left for you around here, anyway. A boat is waiting for you, on the Potomac. I'll have another car spotted for you down near Alexandria. Ripper has all the information."

Bolan said, "Thanks."

"You're thanking me? Listen ... I just wish there was some way to publicly acknowledge our debt of gratitude to *you*, man. When I brief the President on all this, I'm sure he'll want to make *some* acknowledgement. Maybe, uh, an IOU, to be honored at a later—"

Bolan said, "Hell no, don't give me that. I just got rid of one."

The men grinned and shook hands. Bolan grabbed Claudia and left her with one hell of a kiss, and then he was out the back door and sliding into the limousine behind Ripper Dan Aliotto.

"They tell me you're a hell of a wheelman," he told the grinning driver.

"Just tell me where you want to go, Mr. Bolan."

Just tell him where he wanted to go. Bolan sighed wearily and told the little guy, "Just take me out of hell, Ripper."

Aliotto assured him that he would do just that.

But Mack Bolan knew better.

There were no trails out of hell.

They were moving smoothly out of the drive and onto Massachusetts Avenue. Bolan began getting into the clothing which had been provided for him. He said, "Which way to the front, Ripper?"

Their eyes clashed in the mirror. Ripper Dan told the Executioner, "Hell, the front is everywhere. You know that."

Yeah. Bolan knew. And the hellfire trail extended in every direction from wherever he happened to be. One grim fact was always a certainty: always, for *the Executioner*, a new battlefront loomed across every horizon.

He thought of Washington, and of the men who tried despite staggering pressures to meet the terrible responsibilities forever present there.

Mack Bolan had not discharged any IOU's, and he knew that. Some debts never got paid. "Take me there, Ripper," he told the ex-*Mafioso*.

"There where?"

"To the next front."

"That's where we're headed. I thought you knew."

Bolan chuckled, and released Ripper Dan's eyes, and closed his own, and sank back into the comfort of the plush upholstery.

Sure he knew.

He always knew.

That, it seemed, was forever where Mack Bolan was headed.